Lewis Alexis
"Confessions"

Mo Ougouadfel

authorHOUSE®

AuthorHouse™ UK
1663 Liberty Drive
Bloomington, IN 47403 USA
www.authorhouse.co.uk
Phone: 0800 047 8203 (Domestic TFN)
  +44 1908 723714 (International)

Drawing by Mme Eva Koszeghy
Edited by Mr Mohamed Toumi

Published by AuthorHouse 12/30/2019

ISBN: 978-1-7283-9697-2 (sc)
ISBN: 978-1-7283-9698-9 (hc)
ISBN: 978-1-7283-9696-5 (e)

Print information available on the last page.

The author has tried to recreate events, locales and conversations from her memories of them. In order to maintain their anonymity in some instances, the author has changed the names of individuals and places. Some identifying characteristics have changed and also details such as physical properties, occupations and places of residence. Any resemblance to actual persons, living or dead, or actual events is purely coincidental.

This book is printed on acid-free paper.

It was never meant to be a book. I guess Lewis Alexis's life inspired me a lot. He became part of me; his thoughts matched with my words to find a particular meaning of life, to find where his freedom lay. I sometimes wonder whether life is possible with a lack of ambition, despair, and lassitude. An Algerian broken heart, the victim of his own destiny, he ran away from his land and defied the purpose of his existence; it's in London that he landed. He became an adventurer, seeking peace of mind and questioning everything on his way in order to find the home of his own faith. Whether what he did was wrong or right, no one knows; it was his way.

Chapter 1

"Better to have a moment in a lifetime than
a lifetime without any moment."

"You see that couple over there? The guy is so into the game, paying too much attention to everything he does or says. Well-dressed, I must say. I bet he spent hours fixing his tie, and he has no intention of taking it off. See how hot it is in here?"

"Hell yes."

"He's dressed to impress. He avoids using his hands while talking; like a sage, he produces words with delicacy. The charming smile is part of the whole game. But! I say *but*. The girl seems to dominate; therefore, he's the dominated! I don't see the point in showing off."

"Why do you think so?"

"Look! Her glass of champagne is on the table. She's crossed her hands and leaned into the back of her chair, creating distance. She seems careless. She knows she has power. The guy, on the other hand, is almost in the middle of the table. He's chasing her. She's listening to his speech but doesn't give a fuck. Her eyes never meet his. She's distracted by movement around her, the waiters, the music, and her makeup. Now he has to give her a refill without being asked—not because he's gallant, but he has to bend before her like a servant. He's making such an effort. Conclusion: either she's seeing him for the first and last time, or she's staying with him for his money. The guy won't care as long as he has that beauty by his side. He's losing the game anyway. What a man can do for beauty or sex? I don't know."

"Forget it, retard," Aylin objected.

"It's silly, though. Beauty and money," Lewis added.

1

"Hi, guys! Welcome to Vermora! What can I get you tonight?" the waitress said.

"Well, I'd like something to make me happy," Lewis retorted.

"Our menu is the best for that."

"I was expecting that answer. I actually hate menus."

Aylin gave him a cold look. She was embarrassed and tired of his stupid jokes. He smiled and waited for the waitress to respond.

"Oh, well. What do you like sir?" said the waitress.

"I like surprises. Good surprises."

"Shut up!" Aylin demurred. "Sorry, he's being a retard. I'd like to have your soup of the day and a mixed salad. To drink, I think we'll have a bottle of white wine; a sauvignon would be good. Thank you."

"Noted. And for you, sir?"

"Let's be a bit more serious. I would like something tasty and enjoyable. Something I'll eat and not regret. I don't like chicken breast, I'm not a big fan of fish, and I hate mango. What would you suggest? I wouldn't mind some spices to make the experience unique. Make sure it is not too sweet; otherwise I won't behave …" He smiled.

Aylin said, "Please get him a steak, medium cooked, and some fries. You cannot go wrong with that. This is what I call being serious. Thank you, and sorry for that."

"Oh! You're welcome. You made my life easier," Lewis said sarcastically.

"Not to worry. Anything else? Maybe water?"

"Oh, water! We will take a bottle of still water, please," Lewis said.

Lewis gave her a smile, and the waitress ran past the busy tables to put in the order, but Aylin was repulsed. She stared through the window. "Do you think it's funny?" she said.

"I was trying to be, but you didn't let me. These people are part of our world. They're here to participate in everything we're doing, to share every moment. The waitress is not my slave to be given an order to, to serve me and leave without a word. They get bored here because most of the customers are boring and rude. What I do is not for my own ego. I'm happy where I am now; I don't need anybody else. The point is these people are not just bartenders or waiters. They're human beings, and they enjoy meeting cool people. Whether it's a joke or a serious conversation, in any case, they always feel better when they get a certain attention from customers. They'd feel like working *with* you, not *for* you. You give them a better time."

"Look who's talking! Anyway, how have you been?"

Lewis replied, "I'm still alive. I've been a little sick and had to stay in bed for a while. Bed was the best remedy, I thought. Either you recover and regenerate all your strength, or you prepare your path for death to come and take you. Never came, that bitch!"

"Oh! Because you're lucky enough to die."

"I know I'm not lucky. Forget it. I miss you. You keep leaving and coming back. I haven't heard from you much. What's wrong?"

"Oh, nothing," Aylin said. "Just exams coming up. And I did call you a few times, but you didn't pick up."

"Maybe I was sleeping. We have two different concepts of time."

"Can I ask you something?" she said.

"Yes, of course."

"Would you go back in time if you had the chance?"

"No, I wouldn't."

"I mean if you had the opportunity to go back to a certain point in time, if there was a way, would you do it?"

"No! I still wouldn't."

"To change a few things?" Aylin pressed.

"I don't think it's necessary. We should learn to live with what our past has made of us. Besides, going back into the past would only increase the chances of having a more painful life."

"How is that? You could correct the wrong deeds and make the right decisions."

"The only reason you'd go back into the past would be to avoid having all the trouble you've had so far, to avoid that pain you've experienced. However, in case it happens that you go back in time, there could of course be the possibility of, one, living the same life again; two, changing it to a better life; and three, changing it to a worse one. You still don't know. One chance out of three seems risky."

"Why worse? You'd be controlling it."

"No, Aylin! You wouldn't be controlling anything. Sometimes making a decision is like entering a highway where you cannot turn back. The decisions you've made so far could be the best."

"You're so pessimistic."

"I probably am. But what I'm trying to say is I do believe in change for the better. I just don't exclude change for the worse. There is always better and worse for every situation."

"You could actually be right," Aylin admitted.

"I would do something to know the future, maybe. It's more intriguing. Escape a few things, sacrifice your happiness for all the sadness you could have. Answer questions—many questions …"

"Fine, fine, stop it. Let's just stay in the present. I don't know whether you do it on purpose, but sometimes you don't seem to understand anything. And you expect me to be more explicit."

"Well, then, if you have something to tell me, just spit it out."

"Nothing important. But I still want to change something."

"What is it that you want to change?" Lewis asked. "You know you wouldn't be here otherwise!

"I'm glad I'm here, eating with a retard like you."

"Ha ha! Better a sincere and retarded best friend than a ruthless asshole boyfriend."

They both laughed. They certainly laughed at themselves—their faith, and their past, present, and future. They knew how important those steps in the past were. They wanted to expect something for that present, or any future to come—something much better and clearer.

The food arrived. The waitress delicately set the plates down on the table and wished them both *bon appétit*. The bottle of wine was open and served in tall, fashionable glasses. They tasted the food and were quite happy. They gave a toast to those who were not present and drank to their health. The rest of the afternoon was wise and smooth. They discussed the situation in the Middle East and North Africa, which they also called the Arab spring. Lewis didn't take it too seriously. In fact, he never took anything seriously. *Arabs come to life, and Arabs die*, he thought.

"Why would I try to explain things they've done to themselves? Well, maybe not all of them are responsible for it, but some of them are, if not most of them. Anybody who has the same power would have committed the same cruelties, if not worse. They're the same people, the same race. They're brothers and sisters, and they still kill each other. Ghoulishness! I'm not a big fan of this subject."

4

There were tons of other things they could have talked about. Because they were trying to talk about something specific, nothing actually surfaced. After a while, once they had finished eating, Lewis checked the time and asked for the bill. Aylin wanted to pay, but he didn't let her. Instead, she put some change in the tip tray.

"Ready to go?" Lewis said. He had to meet up with a friend. He gave her a big hug and a kiss on the forehead. "Give me a call later, okay?"

"Just make sure you answer your phone."

He smiled and ran out the door.

He felt happy. He'd just spent a wonderful time with his best friend. He felt different with her. His heartbeat was linear, his desires were calm, and his mind was at rest. He was himself. He told her almost everything about himself. He talked to her about girls, alcohol, and most of his stupid comedies. He felt real with her.

The truth about Lewis's life—and there was no use denying it—was that once Aylin had left that day, like every other day, it felt as if a ton of bricks had fallen on him. He was constantly overcome by a feeling of great loneliness. Even with plenty of people around him, he felt as if he was the last person on Earth. No doubt that was probably the aftershocks of a breakup or a betrayal. Life had betrayed him. He'd tried hard to pull himself out of that situation, regain his balance, and think about what he was going to do next. He never managed. Things were going slow at work, he felt like he'd never be able to achieve his aims, and gloom hovered on the horizon. His body appeared not to miss the element of frustration, and he couldn't find the energy to fight back. Therefore, he created a world of his own. He needed to drink. Alcohol became his best companion, and women were a means of entertainment. Apparently, both numbed the pain that resided in his heart. He grabbed his phone and called his Algerian friend Ben.

"Hi, Ben! How are you? I just had some lunch with Aylin. I'm not feeling quite well. I need a drink."

"What's wrong?"

"I need a drink."

"Right! I wish I could join you, man, but I'm about to start my shift. I'm working all night."

"Can't you call in sick?" Lewis asked.

"I've done that twice this month. Besides, I'm already here. The boss saw me."

"Fuck him, man."

Ben said, "You'd never be able to imagine the things I wish I could do to him. I hate him. Last time, I put some oven spray in his food."

"Ha! Are you crazy? You could kill him."

"Who cares? He's an ass."

"Anyway, I'll speak to you soon then."

"Ciao."

London: a dream of a dreamer. Antonio, one of Lewis's friends, had stayed in London for about ten years and never left the city. He spent all his holidays in London, in the area where he lived and worked. Around a few drinks, they discussed the beauty and the challenges the capital had always offered. The question needed to be asked, yet they each had their own reasoning.

"Antonio! Why don't you go somewhere else on holiday to rest, for a change? Why do you always stay around here?"

"Don't be silly. There are millions of people in the world who'd give anything to come to London for a holiday. I'm on holiday, and I'm in London. Besides, you can only enjoy this city when you're not working. I love it when I'm free."

That was the beauty of London, indeed. He could feel the taste of freedom spreading all over the place. He could also feel the strong smell of alcohol in the air, mixed with perfumes worn by the most beautiful girls on the planet. No one was English; people had come from other parts of the world for one reason or another.

Lewis had lived in illusions back in Algeria, a futureless life. Like everyone there, he'd lived for one and only one reason: to leave the country. He couldn't fit in that particular type of society, the politics and, most of all, the religious system. He'd lived in his own world and dreamed of an uncertain lifestyle. Escaping from Algeria had been a miracle.

Everyone has an idea about what Algeria was like. Who cared if there was a sea that people could not freely cross? Who cared if there was a rich desert, or if the population was poor because of it? Who cared if there were mountains that were really just rocks? Who cared if nature was beautiful when the faces of people were ugly? It was an ugly social atmosphere, a society in which the corrupt tyrants held power over miserable, homeless people. It was a society where a liter of water was more expensive than a liter of gasoline. Just like other third world countries, nobody would want to live there—not for the sun or for the beauty of its land. Freedom had to be pursued, leaving behind the dearest family and friends—and a heart he could never find.

People from third world countries risk their lives to a world of uncertainties, called western countries, a real gamble. With no guarantee of any kind of better life. Some of them die trying to reach them. What could possibly push someone to a suicidal mission? Those who know would feel pain, those who do not must do their research. There is no worse than hunger in life, but there is survival, it is instinctive.

Lewis couldn't be bothered to go all the way to his favorite bars. He went into the first one he found on his way. It had never been a problem to find one; there were more bars than coffee shops and restaurants combined.

He sat down, ordered a few shots, and asked for a pen and paper. He had the urge to write. His eyes and ears were closed. He couldn't hear the music playing, and he couldn't see who was sitting next to him. On the sheet of paper, he tried to express himself like he'd never done to anybody. A moment later, he stopped writing. He couldn't find anything else to add. The moment had gone.

A female voice came into his ear. "What are you writing?"

"I don't know. You can read it, if you want."

"Really? Okay!" She smiled.

He drank a shot, looked at the paper between his hands, and handed it over. The girl was alone by the bar. He didn't know how she'd got there, or when. He thought he had no reason to ask her. She started reading as soon as she received the paper.

The routine took the throne. It spread its tyranny all over the place. I had no choice but to obey and bend like a slave to a lifestyle for which I'd never wished. It woke me up in the morning; it took me to work and then to drinks at night. Those activities became a must but were not a hobby I fully enjoyed. Whenever I pursued the shadow of change, I got dragged back into a more miserable state of mind. Some people might manage to escape, sometimes involuntarily, absorbed by an external power, the supernatural,

7

or their unconscious. It's when you lose control over yourself that you lose your reason. You close your eyes and follow a path full of surprises. The story is a tale of true thinking while you witness the things that happen to you. It happened once in the past, and it's when you forget that memory that it gets refreshed by a simple glance, a simple smile, the unexpected stimulus. To be bewitched is surely unbelievable but factually irresistible.

Like a man in a coma, I heard the world talk. I saw images I couldn't get my eyes off. I understood my destiny was not in my hands. I understood the unexpected had come to change my life exactly when I ceased believing in it. I felt a presence, and that presence has populated the homes of my body. They all had the same face: traveling, running through my veins, creating premature ventricular contractions. The emotion grew until my energy fused with another one that was similar to mine, or seemed to be. It had the best features the greatest painter could ever draw. It was life. A life full of impact, dramatic, mortal, even phenomenal. Yes, it was phenomenal! Everything else had to be ignored. That life sounded like a shepherd composing melodies on his pipe yet unheard by the world. This could be freedom in the eye of someone who's trapped. Being chained outside is already some sort of freedom, like a fish in a bowl. Then words were said, needless to think. Nature decided, like the water cycle. I give it to you for it to come back to me. Then I felt as if the world was full, shades here and there, but they all stayed quiet, like an audience watching the beautiful end. Timid behaviors, charming smiles, tender eyes, and spontaneous communication.

I remembered the dream I'd dreamed—not for my own, but to make hers real. And then time was forgotten; worries were dormant, giving strong pulses of doubt and mystery. In that challenge, I sensed a faith of bravery and sacrifice. Was it to take over the throne? No! My soul said, I'll never rule, and I wouldn't want to be ruled. That soul disappeared, got sucked into a bottle offered with my own consent. Better have a moment in a lifetime than a lifetime without any moment. That moment was a moment to remember, completely out of my old damn routine.

Lewis was not paying any attention. She took her time, and he drank his shots to recover.

"This is so deep. I'm sorry, I've read it twice, but I still cannot tell what it's about. Very philosophical," she said.

"I will make it easy for you. This is falling in love. That's the only thing that can actually change your life that way."

"Oh, now I get it. It's really nice. Are you a writer?"

"Not really. I just like to write."

"What else do you write about?"

"It depends. I write about random things. I write about the world around me, and experiences."

"Interesting!" she exclaimed.

"Why do you think it is?"

She said, "I cannot write, although I have thoughts. I think you need a skill for that."

"Sometimes, you just need a pen, a phone, a computer. Whatever means you've got."

"It's complicated, I guess."

"How come you're sitting here alone?" Lewis asked.

"I'm not alone," she replied. "My friends are over there."

"So why aren't you with your friends?"

"I needed some space, so I came to get a drink."

"You look beautiful."

"Pardon me?"

"It matters how important it is when you tell a random girl she's beautiful. I think you are, and therefore I say it. I speak my mind. I guess the reason you're taking space is because you found nothing interesting going on around your friends. You're seeking something different."

"I'm not that beautiful."

"Well, I'm not going to argue about that. I'd feel amazed if someone told me that. Especially when it comes from someone I don't know. A friend, a family member—all lie when it comes to this statement."

"I see. You're right. Thank you."

"You don't have to thank me. Never thank a man who tells you that you're beautiful."

"What do you want me to say, then?"

"You could blush, or show a manner of appreciation and shyness. It's very attractive."

She shrugged and smiled. Lewis knew exactly what she was thinking. He ordered a shot of Jägermeister without offering one to the girl. He drank it, closed his eyes, and made a long sound of satisfaction. He stared at the girl and gave her a smile.

"I might see you later!" he said.

He left the bar and walked across the dance floor without looking back a single time. He went to the toilet and urinated. After a few drinks, nothing felt better than emptying one's bladder—feeling alive again in the toilet.

He went outside and lit a cigarette. He didn't really want to smoke; he simply wanted to know who was outside and get some fresh air. It didn't matter how many people there were outside. One thing mattered: how many girls there were outside—or rather, how many beautiful girls were outside. He finished his cigarette and went back inside because there was nothing interesting. The girl by the bar was the only one he found attractive. She was tall and had long blonde hair and blue eyes. Her skin was white, and her face was covered with freckles. She didn't look happy. Maybe because the men around didn't have the balls to talk to her. Maybe she had problems. Maybe she had lost somebody. Lewis didn't care about that. He didn't even question himself. He simply thought she was beautiful, and as a man trying to get a woman, he had to have the guts to approach her and give her his best. He looked at the bar. Out of other options, he decided to go see her again.

"Hey, you're still here? I'll have another Jägermeister. Do you want one?"

"No, thanks. I don't like shots."

"I love them," he said. "Can I have a shot of Jägermeister, please? The lady will have a glass of water."

He saw an expression of confusion on her face.

"Water?" She was appalled.

'Water is good for you. Besides, I don't know what else you're drinking. I only know that you don't like shots. I actually don't like getting drinks for girls. When you drink, you lose control of yourself, and then men take advantage of your body. I don't like that. I prefer you sober." He paused a little bit and then carried on. "Just kidding. Can I offer you something other than a glass of water?"

"I've had enough, thanks."

"Wise decision."

She looked at him with admiration. It was a look everyone could notice. He realized she was looking at him the way he'd predicted. He grabbed his shot glass and emptied it. Then he put his hand on her shoulder and asked her to dance. The room was full of people, and most of them were drunk. The DJ was good enough, playing the best house music. The girl smiled and jumped onto the dance floor. He seized her by her waist and lifted her like a feather. The lights reflected on her shiny short dress. He turned her around, and she went down to the floor many times. Lewis was a good dancer. He knew how to turn women on, but he never persisted. He let her go and then went back to her again. He took her arm and pulled her against his body. He rubbed his penis on her ass and then kissed her on her left ear. It just happened. He was so close. The girl's body felt warm and sweaty. Lewis understood that she was horny. He left her thin body on the dance floor and went to grab another drink. He loved Jägermeister, but this time he had a double vodka with Red Bull. He sat down on a chair by the counter and stared at the girl beckoning him to go back. He looked around to see what was going on. He saw a wonderful girl dancing with two guys. She won his attention. That one was wonderful—very beautiful. She had big boobs pulled up straight by a belt. She wore a short black skirt, and her dancing was sexy. Lewis could not describe her beauty. He thought she was stunning, much more beautiful than the girl with whom he'd been dancing. He stood up and went for a smoke. He finished his cigarette and then saw the boob girl coming out. He decided to have another one. It was raining, but he didn't care; he was covered. The boob girl needed a lighter, and Lewis was a smoker.

"Yes, I have one, but not for lighting my own cigarettes," he said as she asked him for a lighter.

"What do you mean?"

"Just a way of socializing with people. When I want to light my cigarette, I ask for a lighter. When I see someone about to smoke, I pull out my lighter."

"Nice trick."

"It's not a trick. I just find it easier to approach people. I'm curious, so I like to know how they process things in their brains. Smoking a cigarette with someone you don't know is the best thing you can do. You don't know each other. You can ask any question you want, and you can discuss limitless subjects."

"What's your name?"

"My name's Lewis. I don't know if it's nice to meet you; we'll go each our own way after this cigarette. Actually, I'm wrong—this is exactly why it's nice to meet you." He smiled.

"Maybe you're right."

"Yes, I am. This is why I'm not asking your name."

"Oh!" she exclaimed.

"I saw you dancing. You dance pretty well," he noted.

"I enjoy coming here."

"What do you enjoy?"

"Meeting crazy people like you."

"You have to be crazy enough to be in this world. Those who lead wise lives are weak."

"What do you do in London?" she asked.

"Well, I'm a wanderer. I'm here to study human behavior and desires. I have questions in mind to which I want answers."

"Like what?"

"It's complicated. Besides, we don't have all night. My cigarette is already finished. Maybe I'll see you inside, or for the next cigarette. Thank you."

He didn't wait for the girl to finish her cigarette. Lewis went inside to the bar to finish his last drink. He felt horny, so he asked his lady if she wanted to go home. He craved talking again to that girl with the big boobs, but he didn't want to disrespect the blonde lady who was going to make his night in bed, so he kept silent.

"Let's go to your place," he said. "Mine is messed up. We could have a drink there and chat."

Chapter 2

"His laziness drove him to a world of emptiness. It destroyed
his ambition in life and almost ruined his future."

That was how simple the world of women was for Lewis. He'd just met the
girl, they exchanged a few words and had a quick dance, and he knew he
was going to take her home.

They stopped a black cab and drove to King's Cross, five minutes away
from the bar. It was only 8:00 p.m. When they got to her apartment, he
rolled a joint and smoked it by the window. He took a beer from the fridge
and started thinking about how wrong things could go sometimes. He
wondered why he was there and not with the other woman. He took off his
pants and his shirt and jumped on the bed. He decided to make it quick.
He kept condoms in his wallet because he didn't like situations where he
got horny with a woman but didn't have condoms on him. He kissed the
girl and caressed her body but did not feel like having sex. He pulled the
girl's head toward his penis, and she started giving him a blowjob. He loved
blowjobs; all men loved blowjobs. He closed his eyes and thought about
the other girl. It was not the first time he'd done that. Sometimes he went
to bed with a girl because he sexually wanted to. At that point, everything
went missing in his head. She was unquestionably good. He came in her
mouth and threw himself on the bed. He closed his eyes a few minutes
to enjoy the feeling she'd given him. He got up, went to the bathroom,
washed his cock, and then started putting on his clothes.

"What are you doing?" she asked.

"I just remembered I have something important to do tomorrow. I have
to finish up something for work and need to get up very early. I have to go."

"Are you serious?"

"I don't like being serious, but yes."

"You son of a bitch! You came here just for this?"

"It was very nice to meet you. I came to spend some time with you, and we did—though not enough, I'm sure. Now I have more important things to do than arguing. I'm sorry. I'll see you soon. Will you give me a call?"

"Fuck you, asshole!"

He took his jacket, made sure he didn't leave anything behind, and left. When he got downstairs, he heard the girl shout, "Asshole! Fuck you, you son of a bitch!" He didn't mind, he'd heard these expressions many times before, and worse. He went back to the same bar, hoping to find her. When he got there, a few more people were smoking outside. Once inside, he looked around but couldn't see her anywhere, so he went by the bar and sat down. Her friends weren't there either. He ordered a drink in despair. Had he missed his chance? What was it all about, anyway? His heart hadn't driven him there. His heart was not beating for hers. All he wanted was to hold her tits with both hands. Open a new land for new discoveries. Follow the mystery of her body. The regular were invaded his mind. More alcohol, vodka, and other shots. More desires controlled his body. He had his thoughts in his drink, and he couldn't see what was going on around him—the empty world with or without the girl. He finished his drink, got up from his chair, and put his hand up to say bye to the bartender.

The girl appeared on the other end. He was sure she hadn't been there earlier.

"Can I please have a vodka with lemonade?" he told the bartender.

"Sure. I thought you were leaving."

"So did I!"

He got his drink and moved to stand next to the girl. Her boobs were leaning on the top of the bar. Without looking at her, he pressed his elbows on the counter and said, "Shall we go for another cigarette?"

The boys were busy talking about nonsense. He completely ignored them. He knew he could get into trouble. He knew they could beat him up if he disrespected them. He knew every consequence of different behaviors, cultures, and minds. He thought about nothing. He was blinded by the beauty of her face, the size of her chest.

The girl noticed a loud voice next to her and she discreetly tried to check who the person was. Lewis was looking in the other direction until he felt impatience arising behind him. She really wanted to know who he was. He turned his face slowly, gave her a charming smile, and paused.

"Shall we go for a fag?"

"Hey, mysterious man! I thought you'd left," she replied with a big smile. "I thought it was you, but I haven't seen you around."

At that point, Lewis understood that the girl was also showing some interest. He still didn't bother asking her name. He hated names. He always resorted to calling them *darling*.

"Yes, I left and I came back. I thought I needed some more drinks. Besides, it looks like someone was checking where I was—for a reason we both know!"

"A cigarette? Why not?" she continued.

They went outside and lit their cigarettes with his lighter. He took a long puff and blew the smoke in the sky. He treated it with delicacy. The way he took it into his mouth, the way his lips pressed on it, the way he propelled the smoke—all seemed like a fragile girl between his hands. He opened his eyes after a couple of minutes and said, "It's so nice."

"It's not that nice."

"It's so nice to be here."

"Oh, sorry! I thought you meant cigarettes are nice."

"You girls always anticipate, don't you?"

"Not every girl."

"You've just demonstrated how equal you all are."

"What's nice about here?" she asked.

"We can smoke!" He laughed. "No, I mean this place! It's the first time I'm really enjoying it. I knew I'd see you again from the first cigarette. I came back because I hadn't finished talking to you, as if I had a message to give you. To come back into this world as a ghost or a crow bearing a soul is the last thing I want to happen. I don't want to die with any regrets. The truth is I found you extremely beautiful. I couldn't just go home and lie on my bed, knowing that a wonder like you exists in this world. I wouldn't close my eyes and sleep; your face would appear in front of me because it's magical. I couldn't be so stupid and let a precious opportunity go to hell. My pleasure is being here and talking to you. I don't mind your silence; all that matters for me is to be heard by the person I wanted to talk to. I think

I've told you the words you deserve to hear. Now, I can go and fall asleep peacefully." He paused deliberately. "Do you really want to stay here?"

Words. Where were the words she wanted to say? Her face froze in front of him, and she could hardly move. Then, as if she'd been slapped across the face, she realized he was waiting for an answer. "Thanks for the words. Well, I'm not staying here, but I'm not going anywhere with you either."

"You anticipate again. I haven't even invited you yet. You're not going anywhere with me; I'm the one who's going to come with you. To the place I suggest."

"Well, I guess I know where you're going."

"Let's make it easy. I want to spend a good time with you. I would love to. Call your friends and ask them if they want to join us. We can go to a strip club."

"A strip club?"

"You will like it; trust me. A new experience."

His favorite game had just started. They went to a gentlemen's club and took a table. She sat down next to him, and the two other guys, who happened to be gay, sat next to each other. They faced the stage. He ordered a glass of champagne for the girl and whiskey on the rocks (the way he liked it) for everyone else.

"I've watched you closely. The reason I brought you here is for you to realize how much more beautiful you are compared to these girls. People come here because they don't see these beasts outside very often. They are hot and wonderful, but I believe your beauty is beyond."

"Stop it! I bet you say this to any woman you meet."

"Are you *any* woman? Don't use words I could use against you. Of course I tell some women, lots of women, that they're gorgeous and amazing, because they truly are. I've met so many women in my life, and I've told so many women how beautiful they are. I guess beauty is something everybody can see. Look around you! Some people get stuck in front of beauty, and others feel the freedom to interpret and express it in their own ways. Have you ever met a handsome man on the street but didn't dare to tell him how handsome he was? You wish you had, and once you are home, you are full of regrets. Didn't you ever wish to stop a man you liked and tell him, 'Can I invite you for a drink?' What a shame! How many opportunities have you lost in your life because of morals that don't make any sense, because of pride, because of fear to be humiliated and embarrassed? The point is, handsome or not, beautiful or not, this is superficial. Nature is wonderful but can be harsh sometimes, if not all the time. How can you know this is the right person? Well, you'll have to try, of course. You have to venture and let go. You have to sacrifice and chase. Make an effort. Lead a life that can take you to the place you want to go. I like what I see in you, but I might not like the person you are. I've been in love. I thought she was perfect and the one, but it didn't work at all. Same thing might have happened to you. Finding someone is not just the opportunity of having someone beautiful constantly next to us. Unfortunately, we don't have enough time, but we have to explore the most. In addition, when you choose, you have to choose out of free will. You shouldn't be scared, because everyone is exposed to this cruel feeling of rupture.

"I won't force you to come on my way. I won't ask you to put me in your life book. If it's not spontaneous, then it's not sweet enough to savor. Now, it's up to you. You either lose or win. Life is like a game. You cannot even say, 'Oh, I'm not this type of woman.' When it comes to making a choice, you can be any type because you'll be driven by passion. So be yourself."

The girls were dancing around the pole, swinging their asses from left to right in a place where everybody got excited. They were sexy—too sexy—and everyone watching felt the hunger of getting them into bed.

Lewis remained quiet for a moment. Instead of watching the girls dancing, he looked at that girl whose name he didn't know. She realized he was staring at her, but she kept silent.

She finally said, "First your words, and then your stare …"

"Well, I'm not staring at you. I'm contemplating your beauty. In other words, I'm looking at you in full admiration."

The girl blushed and looked down with a hidden smile. He moved a bit backward and took a sip from his glass. A few minutes later, Lewis moved forward again and leaned closer.

"Hey! I want to tell you something," he whispered into her ear.

As soon as the girl was about to turn her head toward him, Lewis laid his left hand around her neck, pulled her toward him, and kissed her passionately. The girl didn't struggle; she clearly liked the way he kissed her.

"That's all you want to tell me?" she said.

"I have a lot more to say, and in every word I utter, you'll feel wavering sensations."

The girl smiled and kissed him again.

They forgot about the two guys and left a couple of hours later. She took him to her place around Islington. He asked for a drink, and she gave him some vodka with orange. He also wanted to eat, but she didn't have anything in the fridge. He finished his drink and, then took her to bed. They had sex the whole night, and Lewis fell asleep the moment she wanted to talk. He hated talking after sex. Women always talked nonsense after sex.

He got up late, around four o'clock in the afternoon. The smell of food came from the kitchen. She'd already prepared an English breakfast, but he preferred to have just coffee and orange juice. He didn't like to eat in the first hour after he'd woken. He didn't say a word about breakfast. Instead, he went back to bed and asked the girl if he could use her laptop.

He checked his Facebook and found nothing interesting. Just a bunch of boring people posting shit. He signed out. A few minutes later, the girl came back to the bedroom.

"How are you feeling?" she asked.

"I'm good. I had a good time. When I'm in bed, I just don't feel like leaving it. I also don't talk much when I wake up. How about you?"

"You were incredible. But there's something that's bothering me. I feel like there's something wrong."

"What is it?"

"Do you have a girlfriend?" she asked.

"Do you think I'd be here if I had one? I broke up with my ex-girlfriend more than a year ago."

"You never know. Are you still in love with her?"

"I cannot forget about her, but I think I'm over it."

"You're an asshole, and I don't want you in my house! You mentioned her name while we were having sex. Get out of here, please. I don't want to be with someone or sleep with someone whose mind is somewhere else."

"That's an interesting thing you are saying," he replied. "Let me tell you something. My ex cannot take another appearance, and my feelings for her are just for her. No one in the world is replaceable. This is why I loved

18

her. Now, if you have a problem with me having loved someone once, then I agree with you, I'd tell you to fuck off, and I'd leave."

"You fuck off! You're a dirty motherfucker!"

"Here we go. Well, you should have stopped me last night when I uttered her name. This is bullshit." He got up from the bed and went to the bathroom. He washed his face, put on his clothes, and left her apartment. "Goodbye," he said.

All his days were free. He didn't need to worry about anything; even work bored him. He lived on his own. He had his own double bed that he rarely used. He had a laptop and a guitar he didn't know how to play. The curtains in his room were always closed; he didn't like sunlight in the morning. In his wardrobe, he kept his cigarettes and the weed he occasionally bought. He missed his room and his friends. That was why he went straight home and bought a few beers on the way.

His friends were always sitting by the front of the main entrance. They were from the same country, and they'd come to London to seek comfort and money. He sometimes wondered whether their lives back home would have been better. They worked in restaurants and bars from time to time. They'd get home, cook some fries and eggs, and eat them with the chicken they'd bought, if they had enough coins to throw in together. They'd buy a couple of beers, sit outside, and talk about everything their imagination had to shape.

Lewis always felt pity for them. *What a horrible life they must be leading*, he thought. *They sleep, they eat, and that's it! They get worried a lot, get stressed and depressed about their imprisonment in life.* It was a painful life, living illegally in the country. All their visas had expired, but they'd chosen that life of a little freedom rather than returning to Algeria. Lewis's position was to cheer them up and give them some kind of hope. He invited them out and introduced them to the external world. He did his best to save them from suffering in their solitude, but he couldn't. They were a bunch of dead bodies in living clothes, but he still liked them. They made him laugh, and they made him forget about all those women he was after—or those women who were after him. Sometimes he told them of all his conquests and the way he'd achieved them.

"What's the secret, Lewis? How do you get all these women so easily?"

"There's no secret. As you can see, I'm not the most beautiful man on earth. I might have a charming face, but that's not the most important criterion. It's all about confidence and the way you behave in front of a woman."

"You're right, but you normally wouldn't be able to get this many. You must have a magical potion you're using. Can we get some of it?" They laughed together.

"The woman's soul is fragile, although it's malicious. Some tribes believe that only a woman can imprison a devil inside a bottle. There are loads of myths telling us about this. They're very cruel sometimes and almost uncontrollable, but everyone has a weakness, even the most terrific beasts. A simple cross or a wooden stake can kill vampires, and a silver knife can kill werewolves. A woman can be weakened, destroyed, and controlled by words. If you know how to talk to them, you know how to control them. Not everyone can do that, but those who dare always end up in agony because a woman has the will of revenge. The strength of her evilness becomes stronger and pitiless. A woman cries for a reason, and her tears can be treacherous. Women can drown you even in a lava bed."

"How come you always get the most beautiful ones?"

"Well, why would I go for someone I don't like, someone who's not beautiful enough? The beautiful ones are much easier, anyway. Guys always avoid approaching them, and I don't understand why. They all are scared to be rejected. I'm not. I've been rejected a few times, and it's not the end of the world. I think this helped me a lot. My philosophy is the world is full of beautiful bodies; if it's not this one, it's going to be another one. This is how I comfort myself, and I never lose confidence or give up."

He opened another beer and drank half of it. The weather was dry, and the sky was dark with no stars and no moon. It was simply dark. *Terrifying,* he thought. *But still nice for an English weather.* He finished his beer and went home to sleep.

Once in bed, he started thinking about his loneliness. *Why am I staying alone, if I could be with someone right now?* He thought about calling Aylin, but there wasn't much to say. He thought he'd rather leave her in peace.

Aylin … Love … The heart is a mystery. It hurts to love. How funny is this? Not knowing love is like drinking water without thirst, and knowing love is like a thirst that cannot be quenched. We come out of it, and we voluntarily go back. We love to be hurt. He wandered in his thoughts, and his bed got warmer. He kept processing until he fell asleep.

He usually woke up late in the afternoon. His laziness drove him to a world of emptiness. It destroyed his ambition and almost ruined his future. He still had some hope, though he didn't know what it was. He stayed in bed and didn't bother to get up to eat, even though his belly made weird noises. Next to his bed, he kept a bottle of water he didn't drink and an ashtray full of ash and cigarette butts. He decided to have his first cigarette. He realized he loved smoking. He looked at his cigarette after he took the first puff and smiled. Something was going on in his head.

A cigarette! Always here as long as I have the money to buy it. A good feeling that will never let go of me if I never let it go. Why isn't everything as simple as this creation?

He got up and went to the shower. The water was hot, and he felt it cooling on his skin down to his balls. Yesterday was gone, and it stayed in his memory as a dream, bad and good. What the day itself was going to bring was unknown. There was no drive; there was no purpose. He came out of the shower and started making an omelet.

His phone rang, and he picked it up.

"Hey, Lewis! What are you up to?"

"I don't know."

"Fancy a drink?"

"Have I ever said no to a drink?"

"Tell me something new. Free tonight?"

"I have no plans. My plan is not to have a plan. First come, first served."

"You joker. All right. My place at seven?"

"Well, it's already six. I'll come at eight. Where?"

He didn't recognize the girl on the phone. Neither did he bother to ask who she was. She sounded familiar. He could have tried to guess, but he ignored it. She could be anyone. *They're all the same anyway.*

"My place, I said. Knightsbridge."

"See you in a bit, then."

Luci! The Balkan smell.

On his way to Knightsbridge, he bought a bottle of brandy and some cigarettes. Before he got to her house, he went to the betting shop. He played ten pounds and won twenty. He played the twenty and lost everything. *Damn. This is the problem with gambling,* he thought. *You know you're playing a small sum of money, and it's not a lot to lose. But once you've won something and end up losing everything, you suffer more because you've lost more, although that money initially wasn't yours. You go in with the idea of losing ten pounds. You come out with the regret of losing a hundred.*

He knocked on her door and heard footsteps approaching.

"It's me," he said.

"Oh, brandy!" she exclaimed once she'd opened the door. "I love you."

He went to the sofa and lay back comfortably. "I want to ask you something," he said.

"Yes, tell me."

"Can you give me a blowjob?"

Her face turned pale and then red. She paused for a few minutes and laughed with mockery.

He said, "Well, it's not like I'm asking you to do me a favor. You'll enjoy it too. I'm sorry if you find me too straightforward. I'd be hypocritical if I told you I didn't want it, right? Or if I just kept it to myself?"

"Huh. But you cannot ask just like this, so randomly, for a blowjob. It's rude."

"Why is it rude? You gave me a blowjob before. I liked it and want more. Come here, babe, I'll explain something to you. If you need something from me and don't ask, then how can I know you want it? Therefore you can't blame me if I'm too stupid to get you. I like simple things, and I like honesty."

"Do you think I'm a whore?"

"I never pay you for sex, so you're not." He poured a shot of brandy and drank it all in one go, feeling the alcohol burning through his throat. He felt warm and ready for sex. "Come here," he said with a cheeky smile. "I don't want to be rude. I just wish everything was this simple."

He kissed the girl on the forehead and dragged her head down to his waist. She unbuttoned his pants, took it out, and started playing with it. He lit a cigarette and looked at her until she'd finished swallowing the whole thing. No man could say no to that. Happiness is known to be present in those moments. It spread around the room; Lewis could feel it. He put his head back on the edge of the sofa and groaned like someone stroking a cat's neck. He seized the girl by her hair and pulled her off his cock. He closed his eyes and felt exhausted. It had been a good one. The girl got up and went to the bathroom to wash herself. He kept quiet and didn't say anything.

The girl came back and sat down next to him. "Talk to me. What are you thinking about?" she said.

"I don't know. I'm just thinking about loads of things at the same time."

"Like what?"

He felt annoyed, so he decided to talk about something irrelevant. He could understand where the girl was going. Women and questions after sex. They wanted to know how important they were to the men they slept with. They wanted to know whether what happened was just what was meant to happen or something that could last longer. They always wanted to know whether the man wanted only sex or something else, even if their own intention was sex and not anything else; that knowledge was for the sake of their pride. Therefore if a man was being kneed by a woman, he should ignore her and sleep. If she ever insisted, then he should talk about something random and forget he had just had sex.

"I'm thinking about my future. I need another job as soon as possible. I get stressed easily."

"Oh. Why don't you just relax and enjoy yourself now, in the present? I'm sure you'll get the job you've always wanted."

"I know, but I can't help it. I want a job now, not in a year. I don't want to waste my time."

"You think too much. Look around you. Everything is offered to you. Why don't you just stick to what you've got?"

"I do! But I believe life has priorities. Mine right now is to get a serious job, and it's constantly on my mind."

He felt that Luci was upset, but he didn't care. He'd never cared about anyone except for one. He kept thinking about her. He didn't want to think about her. She kept coming back into his mind all the time. He closed his eyes and fell asleep.

When he woke up the next day, he couldn't tell what time it was. He was on the sofa, covered by a white duvet. He felt so comfortable. He looked around and didn't see her stripped underwear. He got up, went to her bedroom, and saw her sleeping. *She's so beautiful when she closes her eyes,* he thought. *If only women were this peaceful.* He took her laptop and went back to the sofa with a glass of orange juice, having a little break from alcohol.

Luci woke up and jumped on him. She gave him a few kisses and asked him if he wanted something to eat. He said no and thought he'd better leave, but he felt lazy. He thought about smoking a cigarette. He thought about having another drink. He wished that girl wasn't there at that point. He felt nauseous. He went to the bathroom and took a long shower. Women the next day made him feel sick.

Luci got ready to go to work and told him he could stay as long as he wanted. She gave him a kiss and left. He jumped onto her bed and thought maybe he could sleep a little longer. He took another look at his Facebook wall and saw a comment from his best friend in Algeria.

I could have died alone, hungry and thirsty.

Lewis shivered. A flashback—Algeria, where all his past was still living. Algeria was not the most dangerous place to live in, but on a mental level, it was the most old-fashioned, as if people never wanted to move on or never knew what life was all about. It was a triangle of religious faith, taboos, and greed for power. It was a bunch of rich people and thirty million poor slaves of their own ignorance. The worst life in Algeria was the life of someone who valued freedom, someone who'd opened his eyes through self-discovery or self-assessment, and someone who worshipped the pleasures of the present life instead of the one of tomorrow and (worst of all) the one of the afterlife. His best friend back home was one of them— released on parole, as the friend called it. Once you were in that state of mind, you always felt lonely, and nothing could fill that strong feeling of lack of existence, always living with the hunger of tasting the beauty of freedom and quenching the thirst for exploring the external world. He couldn't escape; he had to remain in that circle of infinite tortures.

"Bastard! Don't die alone," Lewis replied.

Chapter 3

"There is a woman in every man's heart."

He woke up around 5 p.m., Luci was still at work. There was a frozen pizza in the freezer. He put it in the oven and ate it all. He poured some whiskey and took a pack of cigarettes on his way out. He decided to go to this Arab place not because he liked it but because a friend had invited him for a drink and to smoke some shisha. Why not a shisha? Why not an Arab place?

"Hey, Mike! What's up?"

"Lewis! Nice to see you, bro. I'm good. We never see you around these days."

"Well, I don't like places you like to go to. You know how I feel about this area."

"Calm down. This is good for a change. Besides, they have beautiful girls."

"A beauty with a culture as such? All yours."

"Why not?"

"Meeting an Arab in a bar who tells you I am a Muslim! An Arab is like a snake that doesn't lose its skin, born with one for life. It's all a lie— lying to themselves, to their god, and mocking the world around them. I don't like to put everyone in one box, but the truth is they can't leave their culture behind, and that culture is archaic, too old to fit in this world."

"You bet."

They sat down by the bar with other friends, ordered some beers, and started talking about Arabic integration in the Western world.

"Come on, guys! I don't like this subject," Lewis objected. "Can't we talk about something more interesting? This place makes me sick already.

I don't like the design. I don't like the music. I don't like the atmosphere in general. And you keep talking about them."

Before he'd finished his statement, a half-naked Chinese guy appeared in the middle of the bar, shouting, "I want to kill the aliens!"

"What the fuck is that? A fat Chinese guy! Kill the aliens?" Mike said.

The security guards jumped on the poor guy, grabbed him by his arms and legs, and tried to take him out.

"I wanna kill the aliens! I wanna kill the aliens! I wanna kill the aliens!"

The big men managed took the maniac outside and let him go. He ran across the main road and got hit by a truck.

Lewis and his friends heard the story. At first they laughed, but then Lewis felt sad for the Chinese hero who wanted to kill the aliens.

Lewis took his jacket and headed toward the exit. His friends followed him, and they went to the bar next door.

"Welcome to Earth, my friends. This round is on me. To be honest, I really have no attachment to life. I wish I could die right now. But to think: to be killed by someone because he thinks we are aliens!" He raised his drink and downed it.

Mike's phone rang, and he picked up.

"Mike, where are you? Come home right now!"

"Baby, I'm in Chelsea with friends."

"Just come home. What do you do there?"

"I'm having a drink."

"Leave now. It's getting late!" She hung up.

He looked at his phone and then put it in his pocket.

"I know you're going to leave. Go on, then," Nico said.

"Of course. Not blaming you," Lewis added.

"I'm sorry. I think I'd better go. She's driving me nuts."

"Who was talking about beautiful Arab girls?" Lewis added.

"Shut up. It wasn't for me. You know how faithful I am."

"We all know. We also know that you're a pussy. You've given her more than you should have. This is why she controls you that way."

"Fuck you, Lewis! I am a married man."

"Ha ha! You know, marriage is like a cigarette. We know it's not good, but we still do it," Lewis said

"Whatever!"

Mike shrugged, finished his drink and ran to the bus stop. He seemed unquestionably upset about leaving his crew, but he had no choice. He was simply following his heart. He was following a path that was not the path of a real man. He was a weak man, a man in love. Was that love, anyway? There shouldn't be anyone controlling anybody when it came to love. Love was to accept and tolerate. Love was to give and receive. Love was to free one's partner from suspicions, free him or her from being insecure. Love was to be there for the person when one was needed, when everything was naturally built on a foundation of sharing and conversing. Love was not controlling or imposing. Love was not ordering or requesting. Love was not all the shitty things women wanted. Love was not sex. It had nothing to do with sex. Sex was a means to keep the human instinctive nature satisfied; it only strengthened the relationship. And with love, it became more passionate and tense. *Love is shit after all*, Lewis thought. *It's complicated for those who fall into it, and it's desired by those who haven't experienced it yet.*

The bar was full. Lewis's mind had wandered around, thinking about what was happening around him. Now he was left with two guys without any sense of humor, and he didn't have any intellectual subjects to talk about. He ordered two shots of Sambuca and decided to leave. He called Luci and went to her place. While he was on his way, Luci went to a shop and got him his favorite drink.

In the shower, he sat on the floor and let the water fall on his body. He was processing thoughts in his mind. He was thinking about love. *What a stupid thing, to be in love. Who wants to suffer in this life? Love means suffering.* He'd seen it in the eye of his friend. He might have experienced the density of that feeling. Then he thought of all those girls he knew, all those girls he was seeing and meeting. He thought of himself and his role in the comedy in which he was playing. He came to a conclusion. He turned off the water, dried himself with a long white towel that he wrapped around his waist, and came out to relax on the sofa.

"Do you want a drink?" Luci offered.

"Nothing more that I want."

"It's nice to have you here again," she said.

"Thank you, but I'm here for only one reason."

"What is that?" she asked.

"Well, sometimes, it's really hard to find the right words to express our feelings, our thoughts. But I'm not going to beat about the bush. I've already messed enough with you. You're a nice girl. The reason I came here is I like you and, I want to be honest with you. I hope you appreciate that. My heart doesn't notify me at all in terms of your presence or absence in my life. I just don't feel anything, although I've given myself a chance to. I thought maybe time would change things inside of me. Time has nothing to do with feelings. When I fell in love for the first time, I didn't have time to question myself. I thought things would be different. What I realized is if it doesn't happen when it's not expected, nothing will make it happen. This is simply how it is. A feeling may grow within time, but that feeling cannot be love, only appreciation, respect, and friendship. My point is I don't want to give you any hope, because I know how you feel about me. Better sooner than later. We cannot be together. I want you to know. Now, we can have a drink. If you want me to leave, I'll leave. Otherwise, I'd prefer to finish this glass, at least."

Words had run away from the girl's mouth. She couldn't move her lips. She'd frozen like an iceberg and was melting in the middle of the living room. Her head was down on the floor, and her hair covered her face. He couldn't perceive the expression on her face, but he could guess what was happening under that curly long hair. He carried on talking. The flow of his words pierced through the depth of her heart. She was crumbling, her whole body on the floor. Tears ran over her face. A painful silence drove her blindly to the edge of a cliff. She was ready to jump.

He moved forward and put his hand on her shoulder. She didn't move. He moved closer. She slapped him. "Don't touch me!"

He moved back, his hand on his cheek. He sat down, poured another glass of brandy on the rocks, and let her cry. *Bitch! I should have let her cry on her own from the beginning. This is the reward I get. I've been nice to her all along. Or I should have disappeared without letting her know?* He was there, lying on the sofa, a glass in one hand and a cigarette in the other. He also figured that he'd just lost another girl in his life. She would never be his lover again, and she could never stay his friend.

"You know," he said, "the world is full of atrocities. The pain you're feeling now is just a ticklish sensation underneath your arm. Get up and be happy. I'm the last man any woman would want to have in her life. I might be a good person to spend good times with, but I'm far from being someone who's responsible and faithful. I can be present today and absent tomorrow. Therefore, I keep myself entertained and live every day as my last. I've got to go to work tomorrow, but I hate that job, I hate my colleagues, I hate that office, I hate my boss, and I hate this entire world. Hatred has taken over power. I live in a dark world, and your tears or slaps cannot make it any darker. So, please, wipe your tears away and have a drink with me before I go."

"You're a bastard. You're a son of a bitch. You're cruel. You're not human. You're a disgrace, a devil. I don't want to drink with you. I don't want to be next to you. I don't want to see your face. I don't want to think about you or feel anything for you. Fuck you! Fuck you, you son of—"

"Stop it! Zip it!" he said before she'd finished. "What's wrong with you people? Why can't you understand? And what makes my mum a bitch? Everyone treats my mum like a bitch. You haven't met my mum! For fuck's sake. You don't like sweet words? I'll tell you bitter ones. Fuck you; I'm gone."

He got up, took a shot, and left the girl on the floor. He couldn't do anything. He'd done enough. He'd made her happy, and then he'd made her sad. He knew that he couldn't avoid it. It had to happen either way, words or no words. *Well, I guess I have nowhere else to go tonight. Besides, I need to go to work in the morning and see those asses again.* Home, sweet home. Peace of mind. He went to sleep early.

The next day, work called him very late. He stopped by a shop and got a small bottle of whiskey. Work was boring, people there were boring, and he needed it to keep going. When he got into the office, he noticed that everyone was looking at him. The boss was furious. Lewis had been sick for the last three weeks. He didn't say a word. He sat down on his chair, switched on his computer, and opened his bottle. His colleague waved. Lewis pretended not to see him. He read a few e-mails, wrote some messages on Facebook, and leaned back in his chair.

"Man! What are you doing?" Karl said.

"Leave me alone, man. Please!" Lewis said.

Lewis answered randomly sometimes, when he had nothing else to do or nobody else to talk to. Besides, he'd never liked questions. Especially when they came from someone like Karl. Karl persisted, and Lewis got pissed off. He sipped from the bottle.

"And why are you drinking?" said Ahmed, another colleague. "You're at work!"

A question from Ahmed, a Muslim. Lewis always thought that religion was the curse of his life as an Algerian. It was a curse for every single person on the planet. It was the main reason his country never found a way to freedom and the main reason he'd had to run away, not to be surrounded by divine spirits. The idea itself had probably turned into hatred.

"Well, it doesn't matter," he responded. "I drink because I like it. I drink because I don't want to be associated with Muslims in life, and to make sure I won't meet them in the afterlife."

"What's wrong with Muslims?"

"I'd appreciate avoiding that kind of question."

"You're such a non-believer!"

"You're wrong! I believe! I'm nothing like a believer of your kind. I believe in myself. I believe in what I see. I believe in today. I just don't believe in invisible gods."

"You're strange!"

"No, everyone is strange except me. I was born naked, and I remain naked. I have nothing to hide. My honor and my pride are to live the way I perceive things. I don't have to be like you to be named a human being or a middle-class worker. Fuck it—I'm leaving."

Lewis grabbed his jacket, his bag, and his cigarettes. He opened the door to leave the office.

"Where are you going?" his boss screamed from his desk.

"I'm out of here. I'm fed up with this place. I'm fed up with all your useless morals, your beliefs, and your opinions. I have mine, you know, so keep away from me. I quit!"

"You won't get a penny, believe me!"

Lewis paused a second, his hand on the handle. "A penny, you said?" He opened the door and slammed it shut behind him. He wanted to have a drink but didn't feel like seeing anyone. He decided to go back home.

It was raining. No, it wasn't. He took a cab. No, he didn't. He got home and couldn't remember how he'd managed to get there. He took out his keys, but the door seemed to be open. He'd forgotten there'd be a girl waiting for him inside. He lit a cigarette and smoked it by the stairs. *If only I could call Aylin and go to her place.* He wanted to leave, but he had nowhere else to go. Aylin lived quite far away, and he thought the journey would be long and depressive. Seeing more people would make him sicker.

The girl was in the kitchen, cooking some food. The smell was fantastic, the house was warm, and his clothes were washed.

"Hey, there you are! I didn't expect you this early," she said.

"I forgot you were visiting today! My schedule is messed up."

He went to the bathroom and locked the door behind him. He turned on the hot water and sat down on the floor. He heard her knock several times and call his name. The last thing he wanted to do was to talk.

"Can I shower in peace, please?"

"Are you okay?"

"I'm fine. I just need a pleasant and calm shower."

"Okay! The food is ready."

Whatever, he thought. *The food is ready.* He closed his eyes while on the floor and decided to remain there as long as he could. Hot water.

Two hours later, he came out of the shower and went to the kitchen. The girl was waiting for him. She was a persistent French girl he'd been seeing when she used to live in London. She came to his place so often that she had a spare key. She looked beautiful in her pink nightgown. She was smoking roll-ups and had a glass of white wine. The bottle on the table was half empty. His plate was not served, but the table was ready.

As soon as he sat down, she opened the oven and pulled out a roast chicken.

"I don't want to eat chicken. I'll just eat some bread and cheese."

"I spent half a day in the kitchen cooking for you. And the last hour waiting for you to eat."

"I do appreciate the effort you're making. I know you're trying hard. I'm sorry I don't feel like eating chicken right now. Maybe later. I've had some harsh moments and am not in the mood."

He cut a piece of bread and a slice of brie and stuffed it in his mouth. He opened a beer and washed it down his throat. He got up as soon as he'd finished the last sip. He opened the fridge and took another beer and another piece of brie.

"It's delicious!"

Before he'd finished, the girl burst into tears. He stopped chewing and then restarted again, slowly.

"What's wrong with you?"

"What's wrong with *me*? Are you serious? Why am I not good enough? Why not me? Why can't I be the right one? Why can't I be the mother of your children?"

Lewis looked at her as if he was seeing a ghost. He repeated the expression in his head. *Mother of my children! Goodness!* The girl was talking and crying. He moved closer to her and put his finger on her lips. "Stop it. I think you're too drunk."

"Did you miss me at all?" she asked.

Lewis grabbed her by the shoulders and pulled her head towards his chest to hide the expression on his face. He remained silent. He hadn't seen her for a while. She'd gotten in by herself, trying her best in every way. She was there to offer him her heart, mind, and body. But of course, he didn't feel the same. He felt bad somehow.

"Is this a yes or a no?" she went on.

"Yes," he answered.

He didn't want to hurt her feelings. He'd told her several times in a subtle way that they were not going anywhere, but he never dared to say it clearly. She hugged him tightly and kissed him on his neck. It was so hard for him to tell her the truth. *Truth always hurts*, he thought. He didn't want to hurt anybody. He was contradicting himself—he knew he was already hurting her. And the more he pretended to be with her, the more she'd suffer the consequences.

The rain fell down, and the windows were open. He could hear people running outside. He could also hear her heartbeat. He felt bad. He got up and went to the bathroom. He washed his face again and looked into the mirror. *When are you going to change? When are you going to be the person you want to be?* His stomach reacted badly. He sat down on the toilet seat and took a shit. He felt lighter and relieved. He came out, went to the kitchen, and opened another beer.

She followed him, grabbed him by his arm, and kissed him on the cheek. "Did you miss me?"

"Yes, I did. I'm sorry. I'm not very good with words."

"Why do you guys always find these stupid excuses? 'I'm not good with words. I don't like to talk about my feelings. I want to be sure not to hurt you before I can express myself.' Blah, blah."

He finished his drink and asked her to go to the living room.

"What are you thinking about?" she asked.

"I need to go out. I'm really not in the mood to talk right now." Lewis remembered his phone. He checked the table, his pockets, the kitchen, bathroom, and under the bed, but he couldn't find it. "Have I lost my phone?" He started to freak out. "Can you call it, please?"

"It's not ringing."

She tried again and again, but it went to his voice mail.

"Fuck! Fuck! Fuck! Everything's on my phone. Everything!"

He didn't mind losing his phone, and he didn't mind losing his contact list; no one was worth keeping saved anywhere. Those he loved, his friends, he knew where to find them anytime he wanted. He spent lots of his lonely time writing notes on his phone—thoughts that crossed his mind in different circumstances. He probably thought one day, when he was older, he'd sit down and read his personal words and experiences, and then he'd give himself a chance to live those moments of his past life again. Not that anything would disappear from his memory, but words of one's youth were always different from the words of one's old age. There'd be nothing to be proud of, no regrets, just the pleasure of reading them again. He sat down on the bed and sighed deeply.

"It's okay. It's just a phone, after all," she said.

"Please, leave me alone. I didn't miss you a bit. Do I have to miss you for you to be here? This is just me. I have no feelings; I have no affection. I enjoy myself with everybody I meet, but not with those who talk a lot of stupid shit."

The girl's jaw dropped. Tears poured on the floor. She didn't say anything for a while. He grabbed his beer and his jacket and headed to the exit.

"But I love you!"

"I'm sorry. I don't feel the same." He kept quiet for a moment and then added, "I'm going out. You can stay as long as you want—just don't talk to me about love or my feelings anymore."

He shut the door behind him and went to a park. He remembered love. Oh, yes, it had existed once in his poor life. He'd obviously lied when he'd said love was meaningless, but that love had left him handicapped. He lay on the wet grass and shed some tears. He looked at the sky and saw a star rarely to be seen above the city. He remembered; he tried not to. Those words were digging in his heart. *I love you. What a beautiful sentence, what a beautiful feeling.* He could still feel it, but the person he'd felt it for was not there. He closed his eyes and stopped thinking; her face was stuck on his mind.

He saw a beautiful rock at the seaside by his house. The waves were huge and strong, hitting the rocks and splashing all over the place. He saw a woman; her silhouette looked like that girl. That girl! Was it really that girl? She was looking at the horizon. His heart shook, and his feet started trembling. *Should I go closer or not?* The sunset blinded his eyes. The girl didn't move. She looked magical. He started walking toward the rocks, wondering whether it was her. Maybe it was just his imagination. *Why has she come here? What is she doing here?* He climbed the rocks cautiously, stood behind her, and called her name. By the time the girl was about to turn around, a huge wave reached his height and showered his body.

He jolted awake. Heavy showers fell down from the dark sky. His heartbeat was faster; his body was numb. Although the rain fell excessively, he decided to remain there. He'd been so close to seeing her again. His body was all wet. He got up and made his way home. He started sneezing and coughing; he'd caught a cold. When he got home, the woman had already left. He took a shower and went to sleep. He thought he'd dream again. He didn't have a phone. No one could call him, and he could not call anyone.

He woke up the next day. He called his mobile phone company and asked them to get a new phone. He went out. He felt alone in the city because he couldn't reach his friends. He thought about going to a new place, a place he'd never been to before. He saw a small bar by the corner of the street on which he was walking. It looked crowded. Before he entered the main door, two girls asked him for a lighter.

"Sorry, I don't have one."

He wasn't in the mood for talking. He went straight to the bar and ordered some whiskey on the rocks. The music wasn't very loud; he could hear people chatting about finance, wars, and girls—many subjects he could have taken part in. His mind wasn't with him; too much to digest.

He finished the first drink, a second, a third, and many more. He took a cigarette out of his pocket and a lighter from another. He went out to smoke. One of the girls who'd previously asked him for a lighter saw him. She felt irritated and went to see him.

"I asked you for a lighter earlier, and you said you didn't have one."

"True. I still don't have one."

"You just took it from your pocket."

"Oh, this is not mine."

"What do you mean?" she asked after a small pause.

"Well, this lighter is not mine. You didn't ask whether I was carrying a lighter. I carry a lighter that isn't mine. If I'd answered yes, it would have made me a liar. Imagine a scenario where I drive a Lamborghini, my friend's Lamborghini. I stop next to you, I invite you for a drink, and I fuck you because you think I'm rich. When you find out it is not mine, I'd be a liar. Would you appreciate the lie?"

"First, I'm not that materialistic. You might be right, though. But you still cannot compare a lighter to a car."

"Well, don't girls always say that a lie is a lie no matter what? Besides, I'm just kidding. I'd forgotten I had one. Sorry. Do you want to smoke a cigarette while you're here? This is to apologize."

"Oh, funny! Okay, I'll pretend nothing occurred. Yes, please!"

He gave her a cigarette and lit it for her. He looked at her lips, her small nose, and her beautiful blue eyes. He already felt guilty. He knew what was going to happen, so he decided to spare her and have an ordinary conversation. He'd just talk to her.

"How come you're by yourself?" she asked.

"I'm used to it. I like people, but not when they share time with me. I prefer to be like an old man on his sofa, watching the world on a TV. He understands it better."

"Ha-ha, you have good sense of humor."

"No, I don't. I'm the worst person you could meet. I hurt 95 percent of the people I know."

"How?"

"I don't know. I'm a playboy. I don't have feelings. I think with my cock. Last night, a girl I was sleeping with revealed her feelings for me. She said she's in love with me. I felt bad—not for her, but for myself. I didn't feel anything like that. I wish I had the same feeling. I wish I could love her too. All I did was leave. I couldn't try; one does not try with love. It's not a click on a mouse. It just happens, right? I keep changing partners. I sleep around like a whore. I'm always with somebody, but I always feel lonely. You want to know more?"

"Why do you tell me that? All of that?"

"I'm just having a conversation, and you don't want to end up like that girl in my bed, like all of those girls in my bed."

"You make me laugh. Okay, tell me more." The girl smiled confidently.

"Right! When I came here, I chose this place because I didn't know it. I wanted to go to a new place. I saw you before I actually saw the name of the bar. You looked so beautiful. You were shining more than the lights inside. You were spreading innocence around. When you asked me for a lighter, your blue eyes pierced my vision. I thought you were magnificent and very pretty. Loads of things happened in my mind while I looked at you. It was quick and slow at the same time. I processed everything in my mind; I foresaw the future. I saw you were hurt because I'm hurt. I decided not to talk to you. To avoid you, I said I didn't have a lighter. It was for your own safety and for my own peace of mind."

"I can tell you're a playboy, but what you just said is beautiful. Thank you."

"Are you serious? All you can say at this point is 'thank you'? Well, sorry. I left my drink on the table."

"Okay. Maybe I'll see you around."

He went back inside. The girl's questioning gaze followed him. She was at once impressed and scared. She didn't move. Her friend called her, but she couldn't hear.

Lewis sat down by the bar, turned his back to the entrance and, drank more. It was never enough. Why had he done this? Was it really to protect the girl? Was it one of his games? The truth was he really liked her. His heart had reacted a little bit, but the situation confused him. He didn't understand whether it was pain or affection. He needed to take a break anyway. Girls were everywhere. He could get anyone, whenever he wished. Could he get the one he really wanted? No, she was the one to avoid.

The bar got busier. People arrived in big groups to enjoy their evening after a long working day. Some came in their suits, and others dressed like monkeys; they called it fashion. He liked that style. He liked both styles. He couldn't afford to dress up like them. He still always looked elegant and loved looking clean. He let his beard grow out a little bit to give it a more mature impression. He was confident enough and playful. He didn't want to work, ever. Well, he did, but he couldn't be bothered looking for a job. He wanted to write. Write about what? Who would be interested in reading his bullshit? What would he write about, anyway?

The same thought kept coming back to his mind. He called the barman again and ordered a shot of tequila. Suddenly he heard a female voice behind him shout, "Make it two, please!"

He paused for a moment and then turned his head. He wasn't surprised when he found out it was the girl he'd spoken to outside. He thought he would be the one going to her again instead of her coming to him.

She said, "I like tequila too. What's your name, by the way?"

He looked at the door and then to the bar. Then he got up from his chair. He preferred standing up. "It depends. Most of the time, I'm Lewis."

"Funny. I'm Sweet."

"I'm sure you are."

"I mean it's my real name."

"I get it." He smiled.

"I like the way you expressed yourself earlier. It seemed very deep. Although you think you've hurt some people, you're equally sensitive and kind, and most probably you were hurt yourself."

Lewis's heart made a premature reaction. The girl had succeeded in bringing back a memory. Several things crossed his mind in a matter of seconds. He paused, thinking, until he realized the girl was waiting for him to speak. He racked his brain. "Maybe."

"I like your sincerity."

"You probably shouldn't."

"What if destiny changes the way you think? What if, one day, destiny will get you the person you really want?"

"I don't believe in destiny. I did once. It's already happened. I no longer believe in anything."

"Looks like you've been through a lot of shit. Is this the reason you hurt other people?"

"I've never ever hurt anyone intentionally."

"I believe you."

The barman served the shots with salt and lime. The girl took out her debit card, winked at Lewis, and said, "I'll get them."

He let her pay and drank the shot. He closed his eyes and remembered her face. The girl was talking to him, but he couldn't hear what she was saying. He simply looked at his drink and listened to his irregular heartbeat. The more he drank, the more inspired he got and the sillier he became.

"I'm going for another cigarette. Want to come?" Lewis asked.

"Why not?"

He took his drink and followed Sweet, heading to the back exit. He could see her beautiful, rounded buttocks. She was tall and slim. She wore a see-through top, and he could see the design of her white bra. Her hair wasn't blonde. He wasn't sure, but she probably colored it. It was short and a bit curly. They got outside. He took two cigs out and started smoking.

"What makes you happy?" he asked.

"Many things. I don't know. And you?"

"You couldn't think of the things that make you happy the moment I asked you, but of course you know what makes you happy. It isn't really easy to express it with words. Freedom! Freedom makes me happy. The smallest and simplest things we do in our day-to-day lives also make me happy. This beer brings me loads of happiness as it runs down my throat. It quenches my thirst, it gives me life, it brings back memories, and it makes me feel real and different. We should forget our greed, and love the things we try not to see. We always find our ego and look for extreme desires and caprices, but in reality, everything is set next to us. Happiness is not common in this life. Hatred and pain have taken over. You don't know what happiness is because there are so many things you ignore, and you truly don't know what you want. Happiness is not being a star or a king. Happiness is to eat with a good appetite, to sleep without a worry, to drink when thirsty, to laugh with friends, to love people, to be warm when it's cold, to help and accept someone's help, to share. Forget about orgasms, phantasms. We tend to forget the futile things and seek perfection; greed drives us crazy. We no longer savor someone's company; we no longer have sincerity. It's a world of lies."

"You're right. Luckily, there are still nice people in this world—fragile souls and helpful bodies."

"I know I'm right. Unfortunately, everyone has been contaminated. It's a disease. I cannot be happy while this world mourns bad faith. I've lost mine; I deny its existence. This is all humankind's doing. And if it really existed, then I'm aware I've lost my place in what they call heaven, so I should try to win it on Earth."

The rain started falling as the fog grew thicker. People were rushing right and left. Lewis smiled. He liked it. It felt a bit cold, so he wrapped his scarf around his neck. He forgot the girl next to him, although her presence couldn't really be ignored. He heard a cough and realized that he wasn't alone. He also realized that the girl didn't have a jacket. It was so common in England. He never understood why women went out half naked during wintertime, or why they liked to wear high heels when they knew they'd be hurt the moment they wore them. All the efforts they made for men to like them. However, some didn't care about men at all—or were they just too arrogant to show it? They liked to suffer after all. *Such shiny white skin! So hard to let her be in pain. So hard to say no to a wonder like that. So hard to accept seeing her feel cold.*

Lewis took off his jacket and softly put it on her shoulder.

"No, no, I'm fine," she said.

"Shut up and wear it."

"Don't tell me to shut up!"

"Then wear it and forget what I just said. I love this weather."

"Really? Nobody likes it."

"I'm not nobody, so there's at least one person who likes this weather. You know, I don't even know why I'm talking to you. If I'd met you a day earlier or in another world, it would certainly have been different. Today is not my day. I'm not feeling well. At the same time, I regret a lot of things and try not to repeat them, at least for the moment. I would have jumped on you, and you wouldn't have tried to stop me."

"Who told you that? I think you're way too confident."

"I can see it in your eyes. I've met so many women in my life. I can tell when a woman really likes me. If you didn't like me, you'd have left right at the beginning when I was rude to you, or just now, as I told you to shut up."

"You're clearly big-headed."

"I'm not. I've experienced many situations like this before. For you, it would be most likely fear. Will you be hurt?"

"I'm not scared of being hurt. I'm scared of being lonely."

"I apologize on behalf of all those men who never came to you, on behalf of that bunch of losers who never dared to approach you."

"You're too arrogant, I just said."

"There are a lot of players out there too. Unfortunately, you cannot distinguish them. Someone like me can only destroy you."

"I understand. I don't see you that way at all."

"Well, I don't believe in friendship between a man and a woman either."

"Why not? My best friend is a guy."

"Well, either he's gay or he likes you, but doesn't have the balls to say it. A relationship between opposite sexes is always complicated. You can be friends with someone to a certain extent; but there will always be a one-way attraction. When that secret is never revealed, it makes the relationship last longer."

"I have no attraction for my friend, and he's in love with someone else."

"Trust me: I cannot be friends with you. You're super hot. In other words, I'd always want to fuck you. Sorry for my honesty. Once I've done that, the friendship will lose its meaning and we can't name it anything else. A couple? I doubt it. Everything will be ruined by then. Besides, for me, sex is a kind of thirst I can never quench."

Sweet looked at the bar and then let her gaze slowly wander to her empty glass of wine. "Let's go back inside and have another drink," she said.

"Hey! Can we please have a white wine and a whiskey on the rocks?" Lewis asked the waitress.

"Thank you!" Sweet said. "Well, I don't know. I wanted to say that life is so unfair."

"I think this is why it's beautiful. Just like you. You're unfair, aren't you? You choose whom to give your heart, your body, and your everything. Whereas so many are in pain for not having it—your male best friend, for instance."

"That's not true."

"Why would you want to be my friend if not to possess me?"

"I would probably like your company and your deep reasoning. Laugh from time to time with you and share some secrets I wouldn't share with everyone, because you might be better at knowing how to explain them."

"What if, at some point, you'd ask for me, and I'd answer that I'm busy with another woman?"

"That would be your choice."

"Stop lying to yourself. You'd stop contacting me because you'd be too jealous to bear it. You'd act as if I'd cheated on you. You'd feel weird. You'd mourn, cry, and even curse me."

"Of course. If you abandon your friends, if you don't answer their calls when they need you, they'll get upset."

"But a friend should never get upset. He or she should understand and make a difference between availability for help and wanting to help. I haven't seen my best friend in over three years, almost four. He still has a big place in my heart. Oh, by the way, where is your friend? Did she leave? You didn't realize! You were driven into my world by your own ego. You wanted to stay; you didn't forget about her. You must feel guilty leaving her alone, and maybe you're happy that she didn't want to bother you."

"There is truth and falsehood in what you're saying."

"I know. It's always hard to admit."

Lewis put his hand in his pocket and remembered he'd lost his phone. He sighed.

"What's wrong?" she asked.

"I lost my phone. I don't know how or when. It's pissing me off."

"It's okay. You'll get a new one. A phone is replaceable. What's not is a heart, a life."

"I know all this bullshit. Well, I think I need to get going. Listen closely. I just have to tell you how beautiful you are one more time. I'm happy to have met you."

"I'd be happier if I could see you again. You have some truth to say."

"I'm a big liar too. I think truth and lies get along together and equally come out of my mouth, one after the other. I might say the reason I'm good at lying is because I know the truth."

"Nicely said. Well, let me write down my number for you, so you can give me a ring once you have a new phone. Let's get coffee together."

"I'll take it, but I won't promise anything. I've promised enough."

"I'm not expecting anything from you, only a call."

He took the piece of paper and placed it in his front little pocket. He wanted to thank her for the time he'd spent with her, but he didn't find any reason to. He looked at her. She stood standing in front of him. *Gorgeous,* he thought. She was waiting for him to disappear. She was waiting for a goodbye kiss. She wasn't sure whether she'd see him again. She liked him. She liked his smile and his big eyebrows. She liked his manliness. A man who didn't depend on a woman's beauty. She liked him because he didn't give a shit. He seemed very challenging and attractive. She was lost in her thoughts; her eyes had frozen. Lewis could see her confusion. He waved close to her eyes, and she shrugged. She gave him an innocent smile.

"It's good to stop thinking sometimes," he said.

"It happens to me a lot."

"I need to go. I don't know where yet, but I feel like leaving this place. I'll see you around sometime."

"I hope so. Take care, and nice to meet you."

Lewis took two steps backward. He softly waved goodbye with his hand and turned his back to make a move. He dropped his eyes toward the pavement and walked in the rain. He wanted to think about it, but he couldn't. He knew she was beautiful, and he knew he could have slept with her that night, but he preferred not to. He took the tube and went back home.

Chapter 4

"Some people are here to love, and others are here to be loved."

Everything was clean, perfect, and tidy. He smelled some food in the kitchen and noticed how hungry he was. He ate like a pig. He opened another bottle of whiskey and drank half of it. He ate some more and fell asleep on the table. He woke up in the middle of the night. His hand was numb, and he couldn't move it. He went to the bathroom, washed his face, and got into bed. When he lifted his duvet, he saw there was a piece of paper with a message written in black ink.

Dear Lewis,

I've tried everything. I've done everything I possibly could to enter your heart. I've never thought I'd give up, and I don't know how I could. I was a slave to you, and I was happy. I could have been anything as long as I remained next to you. You've changed. You're no longer the same. I try to keep one image of yours: the first time I met you, the smile on your face. It disappeared. It's like an angel that has turned into a devil. No matter what, I still love you. I never had the opportunity to show it.

Lewis, I love you more than I love myself; I love you more than you love yourself, you stupid, selfish cunt. I love you more and more every day. I think these are my last words to you, my goodbye words. I don't know how you feel about me, but right now I don't care. I've already made up my mind. I'm leaving, and this time for good. I cannot breathe the same oxygen as you. I cannot live on the same land. I cannot bear the thought of living close to you without having you by my side. You've destroyed the tunes of my heart. You've troubled and shaken the bones of my soul. I thought you'd be mine as much as I thought I'd be yours. I've spent nights crying tears of blood, hoping one day you'd call and say you love me, you want me, and you want to live by my side. I was dreaming day and night. I was praying to every god, even the one you've never worshipped. My life has no meaning; my life is nothing.

Every time you think of me, remember my face and my heart. I was born to be yours. If not, then my life is worth nothing. No one could replace you. I love you.

Goodbye,
Your French Kiss

Did he feel anything when he finished reading? Yes, of course he did. The letter was amazing. He could have written the same letter to someone else. He probably had. *The poor girl.* She must have suffered a lot. Well, it was not his fault. His heart had shattered. His heart was equally in pain. He'd lost his love, and the one he'd found was forbidden. He folded the letter and slid it into the nightstand's drawer.

Whatever, he thought. *We all are in disarray.* He closed his eyes and tried to sleep but couldn't. Images of that girl came back to his mind. He turned in bed. He started sweating and then sneezing. He felt sick. He threw up on his body, on his duvet, on his bed. He felt dizzy and couldn't go to the bathroom. The world turned around him. He could see lights, and he didn't know whether they were stars or sparkles. He fell down and lost consciousness.

He woke up the next day, his head on his shoes. He stank of vomit. His body was exhausted, and he couldn't move. His head still spun. It was eight in the morning. The weather was shit, his windows were open, and the doors were banging against the walls because of the draft.

His body was heavy, and his mind throbbed. He made an effort and went to the bathroom. There was no hot water, so he had to shower with shivering cold water. He went to the living room and slept some more. He heard somebody knocking on the door, but he couldn't get up. A moment later, he heard a voice.

"Lewis, are you okay? What happened here? Oh, my God! Your skin is all blue."

He couldn't hear; he was in his deep sleep. A couple of hours later, he woke. He didn't know whether it was day or night. He didn't know what time it was. But he felt warmer. He noticed another duvet on his body and a cup of tea on the table. He was puzzled. Had she come back? He drank the tea and didn't bother checking who had entered his home. He heard someone mopping the floor and heard the washing machine running. He closed his eyes and wondered, *Who could be there? Well, what kind of life is this? I can't even figure out who's in my home! Who's got the keys? Or did I leave the door open? How stupid am I?*

He finished his cup of tea and pressed the remote control to turn on the TV.

"El Gaddafi is dead!"

He turned off the TV. *Who cares? Nobody cares about anything. His family and his fellows will mourn and cry about losing power. Those who killed him will celebrate gaining power. Just like animals. The stronger eats the weaker. El Gaddafi, Hitler, Saddam Hussein—all these people were cruel. As much as I think that, they were brave enough. I actually admire them, though not for their deeds or their heartless actions. I admire the challenges they'd taken, a mortal combat. They were human beings, weren't they? The whole world bent a knee before them. They dared to show courage and ambitions. They wanted, and they achieved their goals. I guess someone needs to be heartless not to suffer from life's injustices. Maybe they deserved to die the way they killed millions of people. But I wouldn't kill anyone. How can I punish a crime by committing another crime? Besides, I'd just ease their pain and make it quick. Whatever, I don't care. My place in this world is as simple as that of an ant. I collect my satisfaction and consume it when I need it.*

"Hey, you're awake! How are you feeling? I thought you'd die."

"Aylin, dear, what a surprise! Death would be the best thing that could happen to me. How did you get in here?"

"I tried to call you for the past two days, you retard. It wasn't ringing at all. I thought something had happened to you. I decided to come. I needed your help anyway."

"I can't even help myself," he admitted.

"I know, but your talent is either to destroy or heal other people's hearts."

"Don't count on me for the second one."

"No, don't be silly. I have some problems right now."

"Problems! Darling, life wouldn't be enjoyable in good times if we didn't have problems. I have loads of problems myself that I can't sort out, but I'm fine, you know. I don't really have to worry much. I fix what I can, and what I can't deal with, I leave it to time. You just need to take things easy. That's it."

"I think I need a break from London. I wish I didn't have exams."

"I was talking to a friend some time ago. She was complaining about something trivial that seemed to be a huge thing to her. I told her that in this life, everyone has to eat his own shit. She laughed, and she asked me whether I eat my own shit as well. I was like, 'Oh, yes, and I shit a lot.' Roosevelt said, 'Learn from the mistakes of others. You can't live long enough to make them all yourself.' One thing can help you: talk about it. Even if it doesn't resolve any of your worries, there'll be a feeling of relief. This explains human nature. We all need somebody who gives us consolation and comfort. Yes, we were born alone, but each of us has been under someone's care."

"Your exams will be just fine. You'll feel prouder achieving something in a difficult situation. You should never stop smiling. You never know whom you can bewitch with its beauty."

"Man, you are actually making me laugh! See, the problem with me is that I don't like talking about these things. I'd rather keep them inside, even if they irritate me. That's how retarded I am. But you're a good psychologist! Maybe that should be your second degree. Thanks for your wise words."

"You're more than welcome. There are a thousand and one ways to make someone happy. Open up yourself. Repression is very bad. I like to see you smile."

"It's the usual thing: I broke up with my boyfriend, so I'm having a hard time because everything is happening all at once ..."

Lewis held his breath.

"Plus, there are some family problems. My uncle had a heart attack. So, it's just too much pressure on me. I find it hard to cope."

"I see. An entire bad meal. I eat the same shit as well." He laughed. "I think I manage to ease the experience by trying to think about it in a positive way. We're meant to suffer for the things we love. Sometimes you think you'll never feel the same way again. To comfort you, you still have a long life in front of you, full of love and happiness. Be strong and be happy. How many people dear to us have we lost? None of them would want us to be sad even in the slightest. Coping is accepting."

"Do you know this feeling when you're just sick and tired of everything, when you just want to leave everything and run away from your problems? I've started feeling that way too much recently. Sometimes I think, Maybe it's me, maybe I'm the problem. Ugh! I don't know, man. It's too complicated."

"Okay, come into my arms. I'll give you a big hug, and then you can go back home and relax, Aylin. Your problems are someone else's solutions. Go take a bath and free your mind from all your worries. Everything's gonna be all right."

"Everything sounds so easy. I'll try to concentrate on my dissertation, then. I'll be free by Friday."

"Then we can go get a drink."

"I want to get drunk."

"No way! Do you remember the last time you drank two glasses of wine?"

"Shut up. I was tipsy!"

"Come back here."

She stood up, moved closer to Lewis, and gave him a big hug. She kissed him on the cheek, and then Lewis remembered the conversation he'd had with Sweet regarding friendship between men and women. *Could it be possible?* he thought, processing everything in his mind. All the girls who couldn't be friends with him at all, all those girls who'd come at some point, had suddenly disappeared. All had left because none of them had been looking for friendship. *They didn't get what they were expecting, so they decided to withdraw and leave. What about Aylin? Is she really happy to have me as a friend? She got worried, came to my home, took care of me, listened to my words, and showed affection and attention.*

What about his own feelings toward Aylin? She was beautiful and educated. She was full of personality and ready to help. She was an angel. *We don't go out with angels, do we? Well, I love this girl too much to mess around with her. We actually need to be hypocritical toward ourselves to save a relationship. Better to ignore a feeling than lose a person, someone who's contributing to the good things in our lives. This girl is here at all times. She calls every time I need her. She sacrifices and she suffers in order to be present. What a heart she's got. This girl is just too good for me. I don't deserve her. She needs a man, a real one. I'm just a jerk, a cunt.*

"Why do you do this to yourself?" she asked.

"Do what?"

"You know exactly what I'm talking about. You're distorting yourself. You drink a lot, maybe you take drugs, and you fuck around like a whore."

"Hey! Me, drugs? Well, I've confessed to you once. I told you I'd taken some, but that's it. It was a nice experience. It's good to try everything in life."

"Do you mean I have to try it too, to know what it feels like to be on drugs?"

"Not necessarily. I said it's good to try, not that *you* have to try!"

"You know it's bad and addictive."

"I know. You have nothing to worry about. I know how to control myself."

"Why don't you find a job, then?"

He replied, "I'm trying. I'm sending applications when I can."

"There are so many opportunities out there, but you can't get a job if you drink at night and sleep during the day."

"Please, spare me that. Don't talk like my mom. Tell me, how is your sister?"

"She's good, but you're not going to change the subject that easily."

"Aylin, I know everything. I'm aware of my actions. I know what's good and bad for me. I just want you to know that my life is not going to be like this forever. I promise. Things will get better very soon." He gave her a wink.

She smiled. "I know you can do it."

"Are you going to stay here tonight?"

"No, I have uni tomorrow."

"Nice. Work hard."

"I need to get going. And call me!"

"I don't have a phone."

"Oh, take this one; I have a spare one. You can use it. I don't need it."

"Really? Thank you, darling. Come here, and I'll give you another hug."

She smiled, got closer again to him, and wrapped herself in his arms. He held her tighter than he ever could until she started calling his name. "Lewis, Lewis, I can't breathe."

Lewis laughed and then let go of her.

"You almost killed me."

"Time for you to go. Don't stay out too late. I'll call you tomorrow. Text me when you get home, okay?"

"Okay. Ciao." She put on her jacket on, waved with her right hand, and closed the door behind her.

Lewis felt cold, warm, and confused. Aylin was a dream girl. No one could say no to her, and yet she was single. What a stupid man to have let her go. She'd come from far away to seek knowledge, and every day she consumed it, a real student who dedicated all her time to build a better future. Unfortunately, she had to go back home to where she'd come from. *Stupid, damned visas.* A few minutes later, he fell asleep again.

"Where are you going, honey?" Lewis asked.

"I don't know, but don't worry. I'll be back before you know it. Just wait for me."

"Yes, darling, I'll wait. Why are you going that way? That's a forbidden footpath. You know you shouldn't."

"I need an answer. Everything is forbidden for a reason. One of us should go there."

"Let me go, then, and I will get you what you want."

"No, baby, no. I've made up my mind already; the voice was calling me. I need to go. I need to know. You'll have the answer too."

She started walking toward a bright light. The farther she walked, the less clearly he could see her body. The light was blinding, blocking his sight from following her. He ran after her, faltered, and fell down. He got up as quickly as he could and called her name. He ran fast, but he couldn't move from his place. He fell down again and suddenly woke up from his sleep.

He was sweating and trembling. He felt tears coming down his cheeks.

He got up, went to the bathroom, and washed his face. He opened a beer and quenched his thirst. That had been a nightmare. He always had scary nightmares. He always dreamed of that girl. She'd bewitched his soul. She was gone but had never left his body. She was everywhere. His dreams were a call for her to come back, but he didn't want her to come back. Seeing her in his dreams was already more than enough. He sipped more and more until he got drunk. He forgot.

While he was getting dressed to go out, he had a funny desire to roll up a joint. He had to ignore it because there was so much going on in his mind. He went to central London to wander around the city. He sat down on the grass in Hyde Park corner and started thinking about that girl again. He didn't know how to get over her. He didn't know how to move on and forget about her. Then Aylin appeared again, and he remembered. He remembered all about the conversations, the times, and the feelings … Then he lay back on the grass to feel free, finding comfort on the green. He felt like smoking some Moroccan chocolate, but he didn't know the number because he'd lost it, so he had to go to get it.

He made his way, thinking about that dream, and somehow integrated Aylin in everything and everywhere. His heart was shaking. This time he didn't try to forget. He got to the place, saw his friends, got their numbers back, and bought a dozen spliffs. He smoked the first one before he left. He felt high and cool, and then he made his way to the blues bar, one of his favorite places. He got excited when he arrived there. The music was perfect, with three people on stage playing Eric Clapton, B. B. King, and Cooker. It was quiet. A few people sat at the tables, and three girls and a guy he thought was gay stood by the bar. It was Soho. Most of the people hanging around were gay; the area was called their nest. Many people hit on Lewis because they thought he was one of them. He ignored them and never tried to justify.

He ordered a Guinness, took it outside, and lit a cigarette. *Such a nice world! Who's got enough time for himself in this world? People are crazy about money, luxuries … There's no gold better than this beer. There is no happiness greater than the taste of this beer.*

Next to him, two English guys were talking. They looked bourgeois: Gucci shoes, YSL belts, D&G jackets. They were talking about two girls having a pint a few meters away.

"That one's so hot!" one said.

"Oh, yes! Well, what shall we do?"

"I don't know, man."

Lewis was irritated. "I think the first thing to do would be to go see them!" he said.

They laughed.

"Obviously!" one said. "Genius!"

"If it's that obvious, why don't you just do it? Or would you rather waste your time talking about it?"

"It's not that easy," the other said.

"Good, that makes it easier for me."

"What do you mean?"

"I mean I can take my time and get any of them, whenever I feel like it. I don't see any competition around."

"You're kind of funny."

"There's nothing funny about it. I'll bet you a hundred quid that I'll get both, at least a number right now."

"Seen the girls? Man, you're dreaming."

"A hundred quid! Deal?"

"All right, I'm in," one said.

"Deal."

Lewis got up, walked toward the girls, and sat down next to them without asking. He took a cigarette out of his pocket and put it on his lips. He paused a little bit to attract the girls' attention and then spoke. "Sorry to interrupt. Do you happen to have a lighter, by any chance?"

"Sure!" one of the girls answered.

He lit his cigarette with delicacy and thanked the girls with a big smile. "I'll be very quick," he carried on. "I don't expect anything from you, although you both look beautiful. My purpose for coming here is far from being the reason you might have in mind. Some people like games. So do I. Do you like card games?" He'd remembered the business cards he had in his pocket.

"Are you a magician?" one of the girls commented sarcastically.

"No, I just know a few tricks to kill some time while I'm having this cigarette. Well, check this out. I shuffle the cards."

He did so in different ways and used a talent he didn't have. The way he moved the cards looked almost as if he was a card player, although he'd never played before. He spread the cards on the bench, showing the backside, and asked one of the girls to pick one up. He asked her to hide it from him, but to show it to her friend. The girl did so. He then asked her to put it back in the middle, between the others. Lewis shuffled the cards again. He put the cards behind his back, pulled one card, and showed it to the girls.

"This is your card. Right?"

"Wow, how did you do that?"

"Here's the thing. Sometimes we don't need to be a genius to create or achieve something. And being stupid sometimes can mean being a genius in other circumstances. It's all according to a specific group of people with specific abilities. Well, this is a simple game. Everyone can do it. Do you think you can do it?"

"We don't know. There are so many cards."

"Even if all the cards have the same letter?" He laughed.

The girls looked at each other, opened their mouths in shock, and laughed.

"You clever bastard. They're business cards! Now I understand what you mean."

Lewis laughed again.

"Listen, girls. Do you want to be part of another game? You cannot lose the game; there is a 100 percent chance to win thirty pounds. Would you play?"

One of the girls said yes. The other paused. "Depends … What are the rules of the game?" she asked.

"Well, it's very easy. You give me a phone number—either one of yours would be fine. I'll go to those guys. I'll call it, and you answer. And I promise I'll never call the number again. That's my card, by the way. If I assault you, that will be my address. Easy to find me. You win thirty pounds."

"What if we give you both our numbers? Would we win sixty pounds?" They laughed together.

"Nice one! The rule for now is only one number. But it may change if you want to, if we'll have to start over again."

"Okay, take mine."

Lewis entered her number on his phone and saved it. "I'll be back with thirty pounds, promise."

He went to the guys and said, 'Well, guys, do you have the money ready? I just met two beautiful girls. One of them wants to see me again. I said next time, because my friends are waiting for me. But I can join them right now if I say you don't mind, because you have to leave anyway."

"How can we know this is her number?"

Lewis unlocked his phone and called the number. The guys looked toward the girls and saw the cute one answering her phone.

"Hey, I've changed my mind. Shall we go inside for a drink? I'm kind of starting to feel thirsty. My friends are boring, and they want to go home."

"Okay, let's go!" the girl answered on speaker phone.

"You look hot, by the way," he added.

She looked at him with a big smile and thanked him.

"I'm coming."

Lewis hung up and stood up. The girls stood up too.

"Guys, are you men enough to hand over my one hundred pounds? I think I deserve them."

"How did you do that?"

"I wasn't asking myself whether or not I would go see them."

He got the money and joined the girls. He had a hundred in his hand. He pulled a ten and a twenty out and gave them to the girls once inside the bar.

"I pay for the drinks," Lewis said. "It's a tip, girls. You just made thirty pounds and a free drink."

"What's the story?" one of the girls asked.

"Oh, I just made seventy pounds myself. Some stupid rich guys. They tried to play a dirty game. I won. Unfortunately, most of those rich bastards are silly. I guess this is why the world is going so wrong. And luckily, because we have people like them, at least we can get a drink for free."

Lewis remained with the girls and spoke about men and women, rich and poor, luck and misfortune. They spoke about life, fun, and drinks. He kept ordering drinks and shots and smoking cigarettes. It was a weekday, and it was quiet. He could have had almost the whole bar for himself. The weather was cool, even though he didn't care that much. The combination overall was amazing. The blues was flying around, mixing up with the enjoyment he experienced. He felt the beat and moved his body accordingly. The girls danced with hands in the air. They were touching him, one from each side, as if it was their first time to meet someone. Everyone was having a good time. Couples were kissing and cuddling, drinking shots of tequila and Jägermeister. A guy was dancing and waving his body; he seemed to belong to another world. Lewis forgot about his worries. Love meant one thing at that moment: having a good time with unknown people, people he thought would never talk to him in a foreign country. Far away, he perceived a hot girl talking to two guys. He liked her. Her name was Katherine. He didn't know her, of course. He'd only heard someone calling her name. He thought, *Why? I'm with the hottest girls in the bar. Is it because these two seem too easy? Are they not challenging enough for me?* He made an effort and ignored her. The girls were laughing at some funny people dancing like zombies. The light was dim, and the walls were full of frames and signatures of random visitors. The ceiling was low and decorated with anarchically distributed colored spotlights. *What more could one ask for?* He thought. *This is called simplicity, to have fun, modestly, in a beautiful bar with hot women. The drinks are free, and the music is outstanding. Why would I want to leave? Why can't it always be like this?*

While he processed all these questions in his head, one of the girls, almost drunk, grabbed Lewis by his left hand and pulled him to the center of the dance floor. "Dance!" she shouted.

Lewis crossed his legs and spun around several times. He moved his hands like a worm, his legs like a spider, and his whole body like a snake. He explored the girl's body, aroused her, and went back to his seat. He sat down and ordered a shot. Before the shot got to his lips, he felt the whole drink pour all over his body. All of a sudden, he felt sick, and his face changed color. It grew pale, and his lips looked dry. He stayed still, opened his mouth, and didn't move his eyes.

One of the girls noticed. "Are you all right?"

He stood up and made his way to the exit.

"Where are you going?"

"Let's go somewhere else."

"Why? I like it in here."

"Me too, but there are other, better places. I'm off. If you want to come, you're more than welcome to join." He put the shot glass down on the bar and left.

"Wait! Coming!" the girls shouted.

He went outside, lit a cigarette, and sat down to breathe. The girls followed straight away, throwing on their jackets in a hurry. They looked left and right and saw him on the floor by the pavement.

"Have you seen a ghost, or what?"

He didn't answer. The girls hugged him, one from each side.

"You're going to be okay, right?"

"Yes. This happens sometimes. Don't worry. Let's go somewhere else."

"Let's go to my place," one of the girls said.

"I don't mind. What are your names, anyway?"

They laughed together, shook hands, and introduced themselves properly.

"I am Joanna, and this is Edeli. You're a funny guy. You take everything easy, and you know how to transform situations. I was all sad before I met you. Then you came along with your magic trick, your charming smile, your good mood, and your warmth. You made my day. That's why I believe you deserve to be treated right and taken care of. Now, we're going to mine. I have everything we need."

Edeli looked at her and smiled, nodding her head as a sign of agreement. Lewis noticed that the smile was cold and fake. Either she was not happy with the idea of taking him home, or maybe she was jealous of not being able to take the opportunity before Joanna. Lewis got up. A taxi stopped.

"We need to buy cigarettes and alcohol," Lewis said.

"I've got everything," Joanna replied.

"Cool."

He looked outside through the window and remembered the girl from the bar. She was nothing; he didn't know her. But she reminded him of someone when he saw her curly hair, her tan, and her smile. He was shivering. There was only one person who could make him feel that way. In addition to the feeling of love he felt, he was full of regret and guilt—a daily feeling that never disappeared. He'd lost his real life and was drowning himself in an eternal lie. Everything was meaningless: the drinks, the girls, the mornings, and they nights. He couldn't bear the thought of being someone different than who he was. He was a lover, and he'd loved only one person. That person was gone.

His friend Bruno's words came back to him, and there was nothing more comforting at that moment. *Lewis, don't worry. You know, nothing is real in this life. This isn't real, that isn't real, and everything is fake. We spend our time waiting for death to come and take us. Some people entertain themselves with bottles of alcohol, books, and sports. You've got women. I don't worry either; I smoke joints, and I'm happily awaiting death.*

The taxi stopped in Knightsbridge, next to Harrods. He felt pain. *A rich woman.* They got off, paid for the taxi, and went to this luxurious house. There was nothing else to say about it. The couches were enormous and looked comfortable. He threw himself on the biggest one and removed his shoes with his feet. The girls were talking a language he didn't understand, but he didn't want to understand. Why would he? He went to the toilet, came back, and saw his favorite drink on the table. He requested a song, which she played on her laptop, and started drinking as if they'd just met.

"You look better now. I was worried about you earlier."

Lewis took a sip from his glass, raised his head, and spoke. "Let me tell you a story, something you have never heard of before. Behind the story, there is another story, a moral, a lesson that can teach you something. Loads of people talk about it. It's surreal and attractive. In the story that doesn't exist, there's a huge world of fairies, which we think don't exist. Now you're confused, aren't you? 'What is he talking about?' you must say. Now I start."

"Lewis! I think the alcohol is talking." Edeli said, and they laughed together.

"Alcohol is powerful, but every power can be controlled. I don't let it go up into my head. I drink a lot. My body is used to it. If I can live with the little blood left in my alcohol, then I'm sure I can live entirely without it. I top it up with beer and whiskey every day and night. I piss a lot, and my body is cleaner than ever."

"So what do you do?" Edeli asked.

"I drink."

"Funny," Edeli replied. "I mean what do you do in life?"

"Is what I do more important than me being here? Does what I do define who I am? I hate these questions. Do you want to have the same conversation you had last time, just like every other person you met? Why don't you dare asking me something you've never asked anyone before?"

"Maybe she wants to know a little more about you first," Joanna said.

"So know the depth of me. My name and my occupation are nothing of who I am or who I can be."

The girls tried to ask silly questions, and it became a game. He played with their brains and controlled the situation from his side. On the other two sides, Joanna seemed to like Lewis more, went to sit down next to him on the sofa, and leaned her head on his shoulder.

Edeli was jealous; she liked him too. The reason she liked him more than before was that Lewis was showing more interest in Joanna than her. Things became more desirable to her when she knew she had less chance to get him. She looked at them and was boiling inside. She needed to do something. At the same time, she wondered why. *He's not even my type!* she was probably thinking. *I guess we become more attractive to someone when we feel rejected or ignored.* It became a challenge, and it was so natural. She stood up and suddenly jumped on the sofa. Lewis looked out for his balls, and Joanna screamed. Everybody laughed.

Joanna told him how crazy both of them were. She relayed their experiences, stories, and adventures. Meanwhile, Lewis was stretched out in the middle. He didn't think about sex for a second. The beautiful apartment had blown his mind. The touch of black all around drove him crazy while he talked nonsense. One caressed his hair, and the other rolled her finger around his belly button. The warmth of the mixed fingers got him excited. He discreetly moved it to the side inside his trousers because he didn't want the girls to notice it.

"I'd like to use the bathroom again. Sorry, ladies."

He walked to the bathroom, locked the door behind him, and sat down on the toilet seat. *Will there ever be a night in my life where I meet girls without fucking them? Damn it!"*

He made up his mind. He came out, went back to his original place, and drank a straight shot of whiskey. "This is so comfortable. Thanks for the invite, girls."

"Just relax," Edeli said.

Joanna played a song. She started waving her arms, and her body rubbed against Lewis's. He got hard, and she felt it. It wasn't the first time he'd ever slept with two women. He'd slept with three on a New Year's Eve. The three girls didn't know each other; they were from different bars, and he'd met them on the same night, a night of celebration. It wasn't surprising. Lewis was like a magnet to women. He was surrounded by a barrier of energy that attracted girls without him having to make any effort. This was before giving them a chance to converse with him. He was naturally very manipulative. He had the talent of controlling minds. He had the bow of Cupid, and when he hit a target with his arrow, he was the only one she could ever love. He knew he couldn't be with everybody. He knew only one girl had to steal his heart again. That was why he had to find her himself. He had to give a chance to every woman who came close to him. He tried and tried. He ate, drank, danced, and slept with them. No one ever came close to the one he'd known before. Well, maybe one, but he'd had to sacrifice her.

"I think your problem is that you're never satisfied with just one woman," Ben had said one day.

"The reason I'm not is because they just don't seem to be adequate to my taste. These women are not what I'm looking for. It requires time to find a match."

"But sometimes you go out with girls, and you know already they're not your taste. Lisa, for instance."

"Sometimes I feel pity for those girls. They like me. I give them the chance to have me for a little while. You've experienced what it's like to love someone, haven't you? You would do anything to have that person. Now the consequences! Once you taste it, you realize how strong your feelings are. They may calm down or grow to something deeper. I never mean to hurt anybody, but they need to understand that some people are here to be loved, and others are here to love. Unfortunately, the two parts rarely unite."

"Then what are you looking for in a woman?"

"I'm looking for someone I can love. This is why I venture from one land to another, to find the right dish that fills my belly and that I never want to stop eating from. This is how it works. I give you ten dishes on a table. You don't know the recipes. In order to choose your favorite, you have to try every plate. You have to. Then you know you haven't missed anything. And the one you choose can only be the right one."

"Don't you fool yourself. A friend of mine told me this once; we were talking about the same thing. She was sitting with her grandmother, who was asking her about the new generation's relationships. 'Dear,' the grandma said, 'I want to tell you something. In life, when you find your own rice to eat, you keep it because if you venture out, trying other rice, you will never be able to choose one. Then you'll spend your whole life trying to figure out which one is the best for you.'"

"She may be right, but everyone has their own doctrine," Lewis said.

"Sometimes you have to be careful. It's not easy—it's painful," Ben added.

"Pain, sorrow, tears, and sadness are part of the love you feel for someone. And we all need that to have a purpose in life. It's like looking for a treasure, except in this case we don't have a map. Some people are lucky enough to find it easily; others need to search forever. I want to find it, and I know it's somewhere around me."

The music was loud in the living room. The alcohol wasn't finished yet. Lewis felt thirsty. This time he grabbed the bottle and emptied it in one go. Edeli looked at him and suddenly kissed him on the mouth.

"I want some too," Joanna retorted.

"That was cool, unexpected," said Lewis.

"Do you want to see something cooler?" said Joanna.

"Oh, hell yeah," he replied.

She stood up, opened the back of her thin white dress, and let it fall down. She looked marvelous in her white bra and white tiny underwear. She had no fat around her waist. Her ass was round and looked firm. She stepped closer to Lewis, got down on her knees, and opened his zip. The other girl pulled his shirt over his head without unbuttoning it. The girls started kissing him. He didn't move—why would he? He let it happen. He felt heaven and Earth were one again. Another night of amusement and fantasy was added to his diary. They made love all night.

Nothing could be better. He had the energy and the strength. He couldn't disappoint them. He was the last one to fall asleep, entangled between boobs and legs on a very comfortable bed. No duvet was needed. Their bodies heated the whole flat. The music had stopped, and the light was off. The entire world was calm and asleep. He closed his eyes and plunged into a dream he didn't want to dream of. How could any dream be better than the reality he'd just experienced?

The next day, rays of sunlight caressed his face, and he opened his eyes. He hated it when the curtains were open in the morning. He noticed that he was alone in bed. He felt a bit cold, wrapped the duvet around himself, covered his face, and slept a couple more hours. When he got up, there was no one at home. He checked the fridge and found some sausages and eggs. He took the freedom of cooking them and helped himself to milk and fruits before he opened a beer. Then he went back to the bedroom. He heard the door open and footsteps in the corridor. He didn't know who it was. He didn't care either. He felt comfortable in bed. He heard the footsteps again, in the kitchen, in the living room, everywhere in the house. All of a sudden, the door handle went down, and the door opened wide without a knock.

"Good morning!" Lewis said.

"Who the hell are you?" a young man said.

"I am who I am. Doesn't matter. I'm a man in bed, drinking beer."

"Where is Joanna?" He replied with an angry voice.

"I could ask you the same question," Lewis replied. "I woke up alone."

"You slept with her?"

"Oh, not only her. There was another girl with us."

The boy got offended, hit the door with his fist, and ran toward Lewis. He jumped on the bed and tried to punch him, but Lewis managed to get hold of his hands. They struggled for a few minutes. The boy saw a vase on the nightstand and tried to reach for it. He finally grabbed the vase and raised it over his head with anger and anxiety. Lewis was there, underneath the guy's legs, looking at the vase hanging in the air. *I'm done,* he thought. He tried to get up, but the guy's hand moved fast. He waited for it to land on his forehead, but he suddenly heard a scream coming closer. Joanna jumped on the young guy, and they fell onto the other side of the bed.

"Oh, my God! Gary, stop! Stop! Are you crazy?"

The boy stood up and grabbed her by the arm. His hand slipped and he slapped her across the face. She fell down in slow motion. The two boys watched her crumble.

"You fucking idiot! Did you just hit a girl?" Lewis said.

The boy froze for a second. He turned his eyes toward Lewis and punched him in the face. The girl stood up crying and pushed the guy several times. With her soft hands, she hit him on the chest and on the face, and then he fell over while moving backward.

"Get out of here!" she shouted. "I told you to never come back here again. And I want my keys back, or I'll call the police! You coward! I hate you!"

"You're a fucking whore!" he replied.

"Fuck off and get out!"

"You piece of shit!"

"I said get out!"

Lewis covered his bleeding nose. He got up and went to the bathroom.

"Oh, my God, Lewis, are you okay? I'm sorry."

"Joanna! Come here, I said," the boy screamed hysterically.

"I said get out, you asshole! I don't want to see you ever again."

"You're a fucking whore, you know!"

"Yes, I am. Deal with it. Now, fuck off!"

Lewis heard the door slam shut. He had his head under the tap and was thinking about the whole situation. *Like a fucking bee. I don't know how many people there are in this whole city. It has to come through my door, into my room, into my bed and sting me. And I couldn't do anything about it. Again, it had to happen to me.*

"Oh, Lewis, are you okay?"

"Who's that hero?"

"Hero, my ass. He's my ex. He used to live here with me."

"You lived with that moron?"

"It was the biggest mistake of my life."

"I need to go."

"Where? You're bleeding."

"I'm going home. I'll fix myself when I get there."

Chapter 5

"You live a moment without knowing whether you'll be
lucky enough to live throughout the whole day."

Lewis decided to go home alone. It was four in the afternoon. He bought a sandwich, finished it quickly, and ran to take the first train arriving on the platform. He was sober because he'd had only one beer. His nose had stopped bleeding. He removed the cotton from his nostrils as he sat down inside the carriage. Everybody seemed tired and were coming back from work. Some people read the newspaper, a book, or a magazine. Others listened to music or played games on their phones. Lewis thought about what had happened. The beautiful evening, then the long orgasmic night, the warm and comfortable sleep, the unlucky end by a punch in the face. It didn't sound that unlucky to him, anyway. So what if he'd been punched in the face? *There is something bitter in every sweet,* he thought. *This is what it takes.*

Once home, he showered, opened his laptop, turned on some music, and jumped on the sofa. He had a new phone and a new SIM card. Nobody could reach him except via Facebook. He didn't sign on because he wanted to be alone. He stayed alone, just the walls, a laptop, a sofa, a bed, a duvet, and himself. He wasn't worried about the country, the credit crunch, the Italian prime minister, or the war within the Arab world. He wasn't bothered at all. He laughed all of a sudden. He remembered a saying: "Life is a fight." He didn't know what was on his mind. Fight for what? *Life is actually a bitch. It fucks you all the time, any place, at any price.*

He went back to sleep for two days, three days … He exiled himself from the world. His thoughts spun around his head. He wasn't trying to resolve any problem; he wasn't planning anything about his future. He was thinking deep. *What a life!* He sighed.

The next day—God knew which one—he got up and put on his trousers. He put his hands in his pockets and found a piece of paper on which was written, *"Call me when you can."* There was a phone number, and it was signed "Sweetie."

Oh, that girl! Too beautiful to be true, he thought. He realized that the entire time, the only person who had been fake and selfish had been Lewis himself. Still, there were things that had seemed real and exciting. Just like that girl. The moment he'd tried not to seek any acquaintance, that girl had arrived out of nowhere. Her wings were still warm; he could see the bright light surrounding her. He grabbed his phone and entered her number, but only to save it.

He didn't feel right about it. He grabbed his cigarettes and left to enjoy the sun.

On his way out, someone gave him a leaflet. *Fifty percent off on all our drinks.* The bar looked nice, and a few people were enjoying the afternoon—young people, including three or four girls. He didn't want to get in at first, but the offer was outstanding at two beers for the price of one. Who could do better than that? He removed his jacket, went to the bar, and checked to see whether they had coffee tequila.

A tall blonde female bartender came to him. "Have you been served?"

"Oh, no. I will have eight shots of coffee tequila and a beer, please. I love tequila. What's your favorite drink?"

"I would say Smirnoff Gold."

"Have one on me, please."

"That's nice of you."

"Great! Cheers."

"Cheers to you too, and thank you," she said.

"You're welcome."

The shots were a warm-up. He got himself in the right mood and called the number he was supposed to call a while ago. It rang one time, one more time … Voice mail. He hated voice mail. He gave up on calling. She wasn't available; maybe it was a wrong number. He checked the paper again. It was correct. He threw it away. *Whatever,* he thought. He headed out toward the bar where he'd met Sweet and lit a cigarette. He felt so good. A few minutes later, his phone rang. It was Sweet. He'd memorized the beginning of her phone number.

"Hello! Who's this?" she asked.

"I guess I should be the one asking. You called me."

"Yes, true, but I returned your call."

"I'm heading to O'Neill's. I met you there a while ago. You gave me your number."

"Oh, my God. Is it you, Lewis?"

"No! I see! So you give your number to everyone."

"No, I don't."

"How can you explain this, then? My name isn't Lewis, and I got your number with your name Sweetie. Is that right?"

"Well, who are you? Maybe I was drunk."

"So you do give your number away when you're drunk! But I remember you were sober when you gave me yours. Should I think I'm an exception, then?" He laughed. "What if I tell you more about it if you meet me at O'Neill's?"

"I won't come if you don't tell me who you are."

"Fine! Lewis here."

"I knew it, you bastard. You scared the shit out of me."

"I'll be there in ten minutes. What do you say?"

"All right, give me thirty minutes."

"No worries. See you there."

The bar was almost empty, the lights were bright, and it felt like it had just opened. He got to the bar, sat down on a high chair, and looked around. People were just starting to come in, and he thought he needed to drink more to be able to ignore the time he had to share with them.

The barman approached with a big smile on his face. "Hey! A shot of Jägermeister?" he said.

"I guess I had a lot last time," Lewis replied. "Do you remember every single person who comes here and what they drink?"

"Oh, not really. I remember the hot girl who was into you. You left her alone here, and she was lost. People would kill for her. I'm amazed."

"I know. You probably think I'm gay, right? But I'm not."

They both laughed. He ordered a beer, and the barman offered him his shot. "Respect!" he told him.

"Oh, thanks."

Lewis drank his shot and went to the bathroom. He peed peacefully.

He felt tremendously good. He washed his hands, tidied his hair, and went back to the bar. He liked corners of bars not because he exiled himself from people, but because from that angle, he could see everything. He saw different behaviors with different interpretations. He put himself in other people's shoes and tried to imagine how he would have behaved if he himself had been in a certain situation.

Forty minutes later, the girl still hadn't shown up. He felt irritated. He didn't like waiting. Well, he didn't care that much about her, but in his mind he was waiting for someone. He ordered more drinks, drank, and went for a piss several times. He put on his jacket and left the bar. He paused next to the entrance to have a cigarette. There weren't any lights in the sky, but they were around him, sparkling like doors to heaven. *Fuck heaven, fuck lights, and fuck the whole world!*

He threw the rest of his cigarette away and started walking, wondering where to go. His mind was full of thoughts and weird images. He walked on the main street toward central London. He felt someone, discreet footsteps behind him. There were a lot of people walking behind him. He wouldn't look back at every single shadow that followed him. Nobody was following him. Why would someone be following him?

The streets of London were very busy. Tourists came from everywhere to see Big Ben, the London Bridge, and Buckingham Palace. They also came to Soho, where homosexuals took advantage of their sexual freedom. He didn't care to see Buckingham Palace. Then he remembered the prince's wedding.

What did I do on that day? he thought.

He went from that topic to another when he suddenly felt a hand on his left shoulder. He stopped without looking back. *Who the fuck is it? I hate surprises.* He didn't say a word and waited.

"You could have called before leaving!"

Sweetie's voice traveled to his ears. He remembered the way her lips had moved when he'd met her the first time.

"You could have come earlier, on time."

He turned his head and saw her smile. His frustration disappeared. He smiled back and leaned to give her a kiss on the cheek. While bending toward her, the girl put her arms around his neck and pulled him closer to give him a big hug.

"I've been waiting for your call. I thought you wouldn't dare. I'd almost lost hope."

"Well, I did! I have so many things going on. My time was not equal to yours; it was very slow.

"I hope nothing serious happened. You have a bruise on your nose!"

"I box from time to time. My trainer is harsh. He says, 'It's through pain that we fight pain.' Let's go somewhere we can drink. I'm thirsty. I'd rather suggest my place. I kind of don't want to see people right now."

"People? Why not?"

Lewis replied, "I don't like people. They're annoying."

"Why?"

"Do all your questions start with a why? There are a few questions to which we never find answers. This is how it is. I myself never bothered to understand why I hate people."

"All right, I get it."

He smiled and pulled a pack of cigarettes from his pocket. He lit one and nodded his head.

"Let's go to my place, then. I live around the corner, and I have work tomorrow," she added.

"Tomorrow is just another day."

On their way to Euston, both kept quiet. Words were too heavy to say out loud. Sweetie walked close to his right side, checking the messages she kept receiving on her phone. It was the most annoying thing.

"Do you have alcohol at home?" he asked.

"I don't think so. Do you have to drink?"

"I need to drink to be myself. I feel good when alcohol warms up my body. Besides, I wouldn't be able to cope with these people if it wasn't for the amount of alcohol I'm drinking."

"There won't be anyone else at home."

"So far, you're just like everyone around. I don't know you, but you must have something special for me to come to meet you. And the alcohol I buy now is to be consumed for another reason. Savor the moment."

They arrived at the front of the building. Lewis lit another cigarette while Sweetie looked for her keys inside her big handbag. He always commented on those girls throwing their stuff inside their bags. *Every time they want to find something, they have to search and mess up the whole bag before they find it. They get annoyed, get scared, and lose patience because they always think, oh, they might have lost whatever they're looking for. But they never tidy up for next time. They like the feeling of suspense and fear. They like to be maddened. This is why annoying others seems to be a game for them.*

She finally found the keys; he recognized the expression of surprise and relief on her face. She felt happy more than anything. "Here they are!" she exclaimed.

"Nice," Lewis replied carelessly.

He faked a big smile to not spoil her little pleasure. *None of them are different. After all, there is one soul in every woman.* The architecture of the building was original, made of glass that reflected the lights of the streets. He could tell from the location that the girl was well off. When she opened the door, he noticed a very clean navy carpet on the floor and two big frames on each of the white walls.

"Leonardo da Vinci! Nice paintings," he exclaimed.

"Oh, yeah, I really like this one more."

Lewis didn't say anything. He stared at both and saw them as pieces of art on which one shouldn't comment; they looked great. "I love art, but I don't like to talk about it. The things to be said are never properly expressed," Lewis said.

"You're right."

She called the lift. The doors opened, and there was nobody inside. The building felt empty and peaceful. They arrived on the third floor where her flat was. She opened the door and turned on the lights. He couldn't believe how beautiful the space was. He was wondering to himself how unfair the world was. He felt like either he was meeting only rich girls, or he was the only poor man on Earth. He took off his shoes by the front door, a thing he rarely did, and asked where the bathroom was.

"I hope you don't mind. I really need it."

"No, no! Don't worry; I live by myself."

He closed his eyes to avoid being blinded by the brightness of the bathroom. He quickly took a piss, washed his hands, and came out. He found drinks on the table and poured a glass for himself. He said, "Sweet! What are you drinking?"

"Oh, I'll just have a Coke."

"You can have that by yourself when I'm not here. Today, you drink with me. I invite you, even though we're at yours."

"I have work to do tomorrow."

"Well, I'm not asking you to get drunk. Just have one drink with me."

"All right."

He poured another glass of red wine, put both of the glasses on the glass table, and waited for Sweet to come out of the bathroom. She finally opened the door in her pink nightclothes.

"Is it time for bed or what?"

"Ha-ha. I just like to be comfortable when I'm at home."

They sat down on the sofa, grabbed their drinks, and toasted to their health.

"Cheers!"

"Thank you," he replied.

"How is everything?" she asked.

"Honestly, everything is fucked up. The whole word is fucked up."

"Ha-ha, why is that?"

"We're no longer kids. Our nature has changed. We have lost the instinctive love we were supposed to feel for our lives. The kids are dead."

"Kids? What kids?"

"Our nature has three sides: the wise, the wild, and the child. It's in the same way Sigmund Freud divided the human psyche, summarizing the whole story about the ego, the id, and the superego. It was a friend of mine who came up with this observation, may the God he believes in bless him. In the front part of our psyche, we have an old man with a long white beard and a white robe. He's the wise; he comes up with solutions, he calms down situations, and he builds up our future. He's the adviser. But right behind him, we find the wild—he's nervous and the troublemaker. The two are always in conflict. Either one wins in different circumstances. At the back, he said there are about twenty children, like a class at school. Those kids are always happy and cheering for whoever wins, whether it is the wise or the wild. They represent our true nature. As opposed to the wise and the wild, the children were there from the beginning, from birth. But those kids are now dead. No one enjoys life nowadays. Life is full of malice and hatred. The wise man is too old, so only fools remain."

"Interesting!" she exclaimed.

"To answer your first question: yes, this is why the world is so fucked. We humans have lost our true nature."

"I kind of get a bit of what you're saying. I don't know, I see something very pessimistic in your words."

"I'm a bit of both. I know the end will be worse than it is now, but I don't give up enjoying myself at any time. I go for it. What is it? Anything. I'm there, I'll do it. No matter how dangerous, no matter how risky. This life plays a game, and so do I."

"Very confident. I admire that."

"I know you like me, talking about confidence, but how can you still want to see me after all the things I've told you? I'm a heartbreaker. I don't mean I'm a bad person, but I've sinned more than I've prayed."

"We always tend to be careful with people who don't reveal things about themselves. Now that you told me who you are, I know what I can expect from you. And I'm sure, before you broke any hearts, you first made them feel great and unusual."

"I've never wanted to break anyone's heart. The girls who left heartbroken were those for whom I didn't feel anything."

"But I'm sure you gave the opposite impression. You're good with words."

"My words were sincere. If I tell a girl she is beautiful, then I think she is. That doesn't mean I have feelings for her. I try to get something out of that beauty. I try to get to know the person, and if nothing happens inside of me, I retreat. Not worth trying further. Then I leave them to mourn their loss. To be honest, it makes me feel guilty every time. It doesn't stop me though. I'll always fight to find the feeling I got to experience once."

"Do you mean finding the same person?"

"Reasonably and emotionally, I know it's never going to happen, and I don't want to talk about it. There are things that we cannot have in this world no matter what we do, no matter how long we fight for them."

"True, because some of them do not depend only on us."

"This is why we have to learn to move on, learn to forget. But we still need to carry on living because our present is no longer the past, whether our past was a good or a bad dream. Through our deeds in the present, we'll somehow be led to our future. We live only once, so we need to make of this life a challenge, a loving and prosperous gift. We humans are so greedy. The best things we do and enjoy are the things we're not aware of, the things with which we're endowed. Our nature gave us pleasures. Once man had created other pleasures to satisfy his ego, he'd made his life, and the ones of his surroundings, more difficult."

"I agree."

"This drink brings me back to reality, my own reality. Alcohol doesn't make you forget your pain, it makes you realize how stupid things are, and therefore you enjoy drinking more in order to make it easier mocking yourself."

"This is exactly why I wanted to see you again. Your words blow my mind. I didn't think that I'd see you again. Neither do I think I'll see you from now on. This is my choice and no one else's. I accept my responsibilities. I'm not expecting anything from you."

"You must have had your times as well," Lewis said.

"In fact, when I lost my first love, I went through many stages of pain. I've known the ground with all my body. I got drunk, took drugs, and jailed myself in my own world. Life was meaningless. It took me long enough—too long—to accept what happened to me. After years of loneliness, I couldn't tolerate a man next to me, although sometimes I happened to like someone. I was scared to be hurt. So I restrained myself from giving because I'm emotionally too weak, too fragile. I feared the second shot would take my life to an end."

"And that would be the end of everything, the end of all pain?"

"I guess."

"It might be. But isn't the proper meaning of life that you have to face it?"

"I did."

"No, you didn't," Lewis said. "All you did was prevent yourself from living. You stopped yourself from being yourself again. All you did was hurt yourself more, because the pain you're living in right now is a pain with no meaning. Blame yourself now, and who else? You try to cry and no tears come. There is no reason to cry anymore. You're lonely anyway. You control yourself because you predict a pessimistic future. You've suffered once, and you think it will definitely happen to you again. Let me tell you one thing: it's unavoidable. At least if you suffer for someone, you'll have someone to blame, someone for whom to cry. Most important, the thing that makes you cry is the only thing that once made you happy. You'll have to suffer until the end anyway; that's a fact. If you have someone, before suffering, at least you can have a good time, feel something, and dream every night. You need to take risks to be adventurous, meet people, and feel joy and sorrow; they're part of your path. Otherwise, no one could distinguish you from a dead person."

"I was waiting for someone to come; I was waiting for the right time. When is the right time anyway? Tell me."

"That's the only thing I can't answer. If everyone knew when the right time is, things would be much easier. And believe me, if you think I'm the right one, then your intuition is completely wrong. When was the last time you had sex?"

"I don't even remember."

"Why not?"

"I can't just do it for fun. I'd feel guilty all my life. I wish I was open-minded."

"Darling, you are open-minded; I can see it in your face. What you need to do is spread your legs. Give yourself some pleasure."

"I can't do that, idiot!"

"I can help. Suppose I'm a man you like, which you do anyway. And I play my regular game. I give you the wrong impression. I can be an angel. You can be crazy about me. I can fuck you as many times I want. As soon as you reach seventh heaven, I let you fall down and crash like a watermelon. You'd be in agony again—something you've been trying to avoid until now.

"The situation here is different. You like me, and I like you, but I know it's not going anywhere, and so do you. So tomorrow is another day. Today, we enjoy ourselves and feel alive, just like normal human beings. The only inconvenience is that you'll want to have sex with me again, but I won't be there. This is not an issue. You can like any other man, anytime. If you think they don't have the balls to come and see you, then go grab them, take them to your bed, and decide whether they're worth staying with you. You have this power. Use it."

Lewis poured some more drinks. He raised his glass and hoped that one day, the girl would free herself and start enjoying her life.

"Wake up! And the sooner, the better, while you're young, fresh, and full of energy," he said.

He laughed and the girl smiled discreetly.

"Come here," Lewis said.

She got up as soon as he asked her to. She tied her hair back, looked into the window glass to focus on her reflection, and moved next to the sofa to land on the edge.

"You don't need to think twice," Lewis said. "Life doesn't always have several meanings."

"I know," she replied.

"Close your eyes and forget about everything. Think about the things you should have done a long time ago, things you should always do when you feel like it. Think of your natural desires. Absorb the warmth of your heart and bring it to the surface of your face. Bring the dream and the hope you've always had. Grow balls like a man and dare to face reality. It doesn't matter what the wise man, the wild, or the kids want. You're controlling the situation because you can. When you look around you, there's only one path to follow: the one your instinct is asking you to follow."

"What about my pride, my principles, and my feelings?"

"Those are selfish and greedy. They want perfection, but perfection doesn't exist. Ignore them. They'll lead you nowhere, only to loneliness."

Sweet watched Lewis speak. She stared at his eyes and moving forward unconsciously, driven by a power hardly understandable. She got closer as Lewis spoke words that remained unheard. His voice disappeared somewhere in the room, as if it were airless. Only his mouth was moving now. She closed her eyes and pressed her lips against Lewis's. She was getting excited, and her hands shook like an old washing machine. She unlocked her tongue and let it venture inside Lewis's mouth. He could feel her fears and her desires. He could feel her warmth and her guilt. Lewis cautiously moved his hand on her waist. As soon as she noticed, she violently pushed him in the chest and back onto the sofa. She got up, turned her back, and put her face between her hands. Lewis didn't say anything. He grabbed his wine and took a sip. She remained that way for a few minutes, silent and confused.

"Sorry," she said.

She put her hand behind her back, unzipped her nightclothes, and slid them over the shoulders to make them fall on the ground. Lewis watched the butterflies coming to the world for the first time. Her body was magical. *What is she sorry about?*

She removed her bra, and Lewis forgot what he was thinking about. He forgot why, how, and when he'd gotten there. She turned around, looked at him, and blushed. She crossed her legs under her reddish thin underwear and covered her boobs with her hands. Lewis contemplated her soft white skin for a while, continuously sipping from his wine.

"I'm offering my body to your care tonight. Make me feel different, explore my secrets, and convince my mind that my nature is more enjoyable than what our society has imposed. You seem to know secrets. Discover mine and reveal them to me. Caress my body like you caress linen. Breathe with my mouth, feel with my heart, open the doors of heaven, and drop my soul inside. Be one with me, run through my skin and through my veins. Raise my existence to the sky and let me perceive the world from the highest. Just do it the way you've never done it before. Let me be."

Lewis got up from the sofa and walked around the table without taking his eyes off hers. The closer he got, the more he felt the energy of her body absorbing the lights of the living room. He smelled her perfume, closed his eyes, and tenderly kissed her. Sweetie fell in his arms. He lifted her from the ground and took her to her room. The lights were off; outside, it rained heavily. He lit a candle and slid underneath the duvet. The shadows the candle made were tangling between their bodies. Sweetie made noises she'd never uttered before. She spoke like a possessed person and screamed like a wildcat. The heat increased, their bodies sweated, and the sky lightened. They remained on the bed, breathing like thirsty dogs. A few hours later, she fell asleep on Lewis's chest without saying a word. He caressed her head, gave her a kiss, and also fell asleep. She was amazing.

The next day, Lewis woke up in the middle of the day. He felt thirsty and tried to find a drink next to the bed. He got up, went to the kitchen, and drank a jar of water. *Nice,* he thought. *I can't even remember when I last had some water.* He went to the bathroom to take a piss but saw the lights were on and the water was running. *Mmm, she's taking a bath!* He opened the door and saw water on the floor. He looked in, wanting to surprise her, but his expectation was far away from his imagination. He saw Sweetie inside the bathtub full of blood. He freaked, his legs shook, and his face grew pale. He was scared and didn't know what to do. Her head was in the water, and her arm hung over the side, bleeding from the wrist. There was a blade in the other hand and a Bible between her legs. He came out of the bathroom and threw up all over the corridor. He searched for his phone and called an ambulance. He went back to bed, lay on the duvet, and started crying.

Feelings! What were they for him? He cried not only for her death but for all of his past, all his guilt, all his bad and good experiences. He didn't stop crying, not even when the police came in. He told them what had happened, how he'd met her, and how he'd gotten there. He wept on the bed, trembling with regret.

One of the policemen came with a paper he said he'd found on the dining table. It appeared to be a letter, a message. "I don't know if this is for you, but your name is at the top, and it's signed by the girl."

Lewis heard perfectly but didn't give the policeman any attention. He couldn't move; he didn't want to move.

"Do you want to read it?" the black officer asked.

"Yes, put it on the bed."

"I can't. I have to take it with me."

He raised his head nervously and gave the man a very cold look.

"What else do you want to take? Is there anything left? What? Tell me! I'll read it whenever I feel like it, and then you take it." He finally took the letter, breathed deeply, and opened it.

Dear Lewis,

I'm sorry. I know you must feel down right now. You must feel devastated, hurt, guilty, cursed, and maybe worse than I can imagined. Maybe you could pretend nothing happened, leave, and forget about me. But I'm sure you're not that kind of person. Don't feel guilty. Don't punish yourself. There's no reason for doing so. You've freed me from a cursed world. You've shown me the path to heaven. You've made my dreams come true. I die happy, with a unique feeling. I've never felt this way before. Oh, my God, your touch, your kisses, the way you breathe, your smell, your sweat, your tongue, your legs, and your arms—everything. I'm melting. I've never experienced this world before. I cannot express it adequately. You've saved my life from terror, from darkness and pain. You've changed my life, and this night was better than any of the whole world. My heart grew bigger. Thanks to you, I know what happiness is. I wish I could stay. I wish what I felt would last a lifetime, but realistically, I know it won't happen. I don't want to take the risk. I don't want to live in pain again, I don't want to feel sad. I don't want to feel alone anymore. God bless the day I came to see you. I don't know how. I felt a different energy sparkling from your body. I could see the sound of your voice waving in the air as if time had slowed down. I can still hear your voice whispering my name into my ears.

I don't know how to describe my feelings; I've never felt such an immense enchantment. It's so painful, a pain that makes me happier than ever. Maybe it's love, but I think it's something beyond that. Thank you very much, Lewis, and goodbye.

Sweet

He gave the police his details for the investigation. He put his clothes on and left. There was only one place where he could go: Aylin's. He couldn't go home. He couldn't bear the thought of being home alone.

He got to her apartment with tears in his eyes, the most miserable expression imaginable on a man's face.

Chapter 6

"We are bound to suffer and only in suffering we indulge."

"Oh, my God, Lewis! What's wrong?"

"Nothing," he answered indifferently. "I need a bath, please."

"But tell me what's the matter. You're crying. I've never seen you cry before!"

"A bath, please. Then we talk."

She ran to the bathroom and turned on the hot water. He heard the water run and cried again. He sat down on the sofa and thought about everything. It took him a while. He was stuck, wandering in the deepest of his thoughts. He couldn't believe what had happened and why it had had to happen to him. At the same time, he thought that life would never stop surprising him.

"It's ready. Come! Oh, my God, I hope it's going to be okay. Talk to me, please. I can do anything for you."

"I know, Aylin. Thanks."

He took off his clothes and slid himself into the boiling hot water. His heart was cold and his body was frozen. The thought of joining the girl, following her, came into his mind alongside the devil. His reason was stronger. He rejected it for the sake of not creating a chain of stupidity. His best friend might get depressed or commit the same mistake. He also thought about the letter and the depth of its meaning. He closed his eyes and let images run in front of him until he fell asleep.

Hours later, Aylin entered the bathroom and woke him up.

"Hey! The water's cold. Get up!"

She helped him dry his body with her towel, gave him underwear he'd left there a while ago, and asked him to go to bed. He felt at home.

Her place was the only place where he could truly rest. He could see peace drawn on the walls, lying on the ground. The fresh air he breathed, the cleanness of the atmosphere, the care he was receiving. *Warmth.* He was thinking about warmth. *Not feeling cold! No, it's not. Warmth is this place, the heart of that girl I want to protect. I never lie to her, but this time I think I need to.*

"Do you want an extra duvet?"

"Aylin, please stop taking care of me. It's too much for me."

"Shut up!"

"Are you busy?"

"I need to study, but I'm here. Tell me what happened."

"Nothing. I got drunk and remembered the worst things that have happened to me. I got emotional and broke down. I couldn't stop crying because I liked it. I just let my tears flow. I needed a place to go to. I thought my place is the worst. Your company, your house, everything that surrounds you—it's like a part of me. I feel at home here. Thank you. There are things I don't want to ask myself, things I prefer not to know. Knowledge can harm sometimes. So there's nothing to worry about. You know how strong I am."

"I always tell you to stop drinking. You're abusing."

"What else do you want me to do?"

"You gave up on your life. This is not the person I know. I don't recognize you anymore. You have a great potential to become someone important."

"Am I not to you?"

"Don't be silly. You know exactly what I mean."

"Yes, I do. I don't know. It's true I have neglected my path of success. I'm disabled by my own will. I've lost it. I've been thinking about it a lot, and the main reason I'm going crazy these days is exactly what we're bringing up. I need to do something about it."

"Start by reducing the amount of alcohol you're drinking."

"I'll try."

As soon as he'd finished the sentence, Lewis fell asleep. He woke up the next day, opened Aylin's laptop, and started writing an e-mail to his best friend Ed back home in Algeria.

Dear Friend,

Sorry, I've been hibernating. You must be very angry, but you know you shouldn't be. I love you, and you're aware of that. If only you knew what life has made of me since I left Algeria.

There are indeed two different paths in this world: the path of the survivor, which is most likely the one of being born in Algeria or any similar country; and the path of the man living in a more developed society. I am just like you, a survivor. Trust me, I wish I'd never seen this world. Sometimes it's good to live in total ignorance. It's very hard, or even harder, to live abroad as an Algerian because the moment you start enjoying your life, the moment you start integrating and constructing your own life, and the moment you feel human, you'll have to go back to where you came from because your visa expires. Your time is limited.

I've tried my best. and I've been quite foolish thinking that I could, at some point, stay here forever and never have to return. I don't know how. My options are restricted. I'm no longer enjoying my time, and trying to forget the place where I came from is just another lie. I've completely changed my way of thinking. Alcohol is my best company; I worship its presence and always welcome mind influencers such as drugs. I guess it's a way of hiding behind a transparent curtain.

I spend all my time drinking and amusing myself, as if my life was to come to an end very soon. Why would I work hard? Why would I worry my mind? I was more ambitious, but now I've lost it all. I've discovered another world, and even this one is a lie. My quest of finding love and freedom is a failure. We're bound to suffer, and only in suffering do we indulge. Can we really be happy? I doubt it. I don't want to sound depressive, but this is how I feel about everything, and it's not a complaint. I accepted that a long time ago. All I have felt is pain, and I see it everywhere. I realized that moments of happiness only last while you experience them, and they're very short. Reality is harsh.

Take extra care of yourself, my dear friend.

Lewis

He pressed send, closed the laptop, and went back to bed. He wanted to forget, he wanted to move on. He knew it wasn't easy, and he was trying so hard. Giving up wasn't the best of solutions; he was on the edge of depression. He always knew how to comfort his friends but not himself. He always knew how to cheer up people, but he never knew how to apply it to himself. His psychological skills didn't help him at all.

The weather was nice, with a clear sky and bright sun, a few birds sang in the garden. It was so calm. The windows were closed. He felt warm and relaxed. He was a bit hungry, but he didn't bother leaving the bed. His laziness had a big impact on his life, and it was a big burden, tying his legs and arms. Only his mind functioned, but what could he do without his legs and arms? Practically nothing. He thought about disabled people when the idea crossed his mind. Yes, poor people. Did he consider the luck of having those arms and legs? No, he didn't. *Everyone's destiny, everyone's fate. Everyone mourns life the way it is. What's the point of putting oneself in someone else's shoes? In order to feel better? Why should someone's pain be someone else's happiness or comfort? What's wrong with these people? Everything has taken the wrong path, and everything seems to destroy humanity. Are they all aware of their deeds?* Lewis had spent all day trying to answer these questions. He could come up with answers to some, but a few were left without any resolution. He didn't care whether God existed, and he didn't care whether he'd ever believed he existed.

He switched on the TV and listened to some music. His phone rang, but he didn't want to answer. He didn't bother checking who the person calling was. He went to the balcony, sat down on a wooden chair, and looked at the sky. It was already getting dark, and so far he hadn't had a single drink. He wanted to, but he tried not to. The door opened; Aylin was home. He heard her heavy heels hitting the ground.

"Lewis!" she called. "Lewis!"

"I'm here," he answered.

"Why didn't you answer your phone? I wanted you to come out to eat with me."

"The world is scary, Aylin. I'd prefer to stay at home, in peace. I heard the phone ring and ignored it. The world outside is meaningless. The answers I get from the outside world are depressive. They're the complete opposite of what I get from my own world.

"Lewis! I hate it when you start your bullshit. Let's go eat."

"Go where?"

"Out!"

"Haven't you heard a single word of what I just said? Aylin, the world I used to live in was peaceful. I've been thrown to this life as if I'd sinned, to be punished. I'm still aware, and I remember those times. We all came to this world through pain, and in pain we all live. Open a bottle of wine and sit down next to me. We don't need to go to a restaurant; their food is bitter, and their people are ugly. I see misery on people's faces. I see hopeless eyes and fake smiles. I see people struggling to forget. It hurts me."

"Well, let's say you're drowning in that ocean. Wouldn't you ever resurface again? You don't need to look at those people to lead a good life."

"Good life! What's a good life? The tears you shed? The choices you never made? The sorrow that bewitches you? I know that psychology. It's the most hypocritical reasoning."

"You've always told me the opposite."

"Because my life and yours are not the same. I'm the meaning of failure, and you're the one of success. You're here in this world to spread love and joy. You're here to help people find their ways. Your words, no matter how sad they are, become inspirational. When I talk to you, I feel happy because I know you're not like me. I know I cannot be like you because I don't like the place I come from or the one I'm living in right now. I don't feel like I belong anywhere."

"Lewis, stop being silly."

"Being silly is the answer to everything. Trying to be clever is the weapon that destroyed humanity. Look at the world around you. Clever men are the source of destruction and war. No matter how big the sin I've ever made, I think I deserve to be living in a better world. I could have been different."

"I'm sure you are."

Aylin opened a bottle of wine and poured two glasses, and they kept talking about the real world and mostly the fake one, spending the night on the balcony under the dark sky. Bright lights shone from different buildings, and cars drove along peacefully on the streets. The world at that point was quiet.

"This is why I like nighttime. There are fewer people out there, and those who are out try their best to get as drunk as possible. In other words, they try to escape this world and live in a different one, to feel human. Alcohol is never enough; they take pills, ecstasy, MDMA, cocaine, heroin … You think that all these drugs make you feel really good, make you feel like you can fly? Bullshit! It feels like shit, it tastes like shit, it's horrible. They like it because their eyes open to the real world. It allows them to finally take their freedom and do whatever they feel like. They ignore taboos, traditions, and religion. They ignore all that humankind has created. They listen to their nature. Hearts speak, ears listen, eyes see, skin feels, tongues taste, noses smell, dicks get hard. Everything we don't experience during daytime or when we're sober. That world is feared because people cannot afford to enter it. It looks scary because people who have been there never want to come back. They look mad, and they've lost their senses. You know nothing about it. Your worries are nothing compared to theirs. Who complains at the end of the day? Normal people."

"I've always known that you're not normal. You're crazy and stupid. I'll always repeat that in case you ever forget."

"That makes me happy. You make me happy by saying that. You know almost everything about me. I don't love you just for that, but because you know I'm an idiot and still love me."

They managed to laugh together. They finished their drink and went to bed. They lay next to each other and made some jokes before they both fell asleep. They looked beautiful, perfect, but there was something that couldn't be happening there. They were just friends. Nothing could change that.

Lewis slept, and he was taken somewhere wonderfully comfortable. He couldn't dream, and everything was blank and calm. The bed was warm and soft. Next to him the most beautiful girl he could ever have. She was his guardian. When she stayed with him, the devil never came around. He felt the need to protect her, support her, and help her the way she always helped him. He didn't know how to do that. He wasn't man enough himself. It was always easier to blame and tease other people. He used his weakness to unveil other men's weaknesses. A night like this was priceless. No one could ever buy that magical friendship, or whatever he should call it.

When he woke up, Aylin was painting on the floor. He didn't say a word. She looked absent in her world. There was love in her paintings, a commitment, faith, life, and hope. He watched her dip the brush in colors and give them life on a white canvas. She gave them meaning inspired by her feelings. She spent hours producing art, at the same time having fun doing what she'd always loved doing.

When Lewis felt she was a bit tired, he got up. "Hi! I was awake. I just didn't want to disturb you. Shall we eat something?"

"Oh, yes, I'm hungry."

They both went to the kitchen. With four hands, they managed to cook quickly and set the table, and then they ate slowly. Lewis reviewed the whole scene in his mind. He thought about love.

"Love is beautiful," he said.

"I don't believe in love anymore," she replied.

"With love, you remember nights and days. You remember joy and tears, times in someone's arms, times when you lost yourself and came to life again. You remember every breath you take, a lifetime in every kiss. You remember times when you had to stand up, had to keep fighting. Times when you had to be, just because of love. Times when you thought you'd walk alone, but love gave you somebody by your side. You remember the peace and war between your soul and the depth of your heart. You remember being one person but then another one once you were in love. Because of love, you never forget smiles and faces. The earthquake that strikes your heart. You could be the stupidest person on Earth because of love, but you always remember, just because the person you feel those things for existed and made you feel like you exist. Love is powerful, Aylin. You never know when it's going to happen. You'll never expect it."

Tears dropped from Lewis's eyes. He realized that love was not just a simple comedy, not like just any game. Love was like chess. He'd lost, and his heart was pressed against a huge wall—checkmate. When he spoke about love, his heart felt like it was being squeezed like an orange. He was smiling at the same time.

Running down his face were tears of love, tears of joy, and tears of misfortune. A combination of feelings that made Lewis lose his mind. His meaningless life had no future, he believed. What was the point of getting up in the morning, having lunch on time, and seeing other people? The only thing that lured him out was the alcohol he drank and the drugs of all sorts he took. For him, staying awake was nonsense, so he plunged himself into a world of Illusions, living his past daily in the present.

He took his glass of wine and raised it in the air, high, very high. "This is for love." He clinked Aylin's glass and downed his drink.

Aylin simply listened, probably lost in the world of his confusions. Was it love he was talking about? "Stop drinking!" she said.

"Oh, Aylin. Love made me start, and only love will make me stop. Alcohol is not the issue. I always tell you that."

"You're annoying."

"It's the best I could do so far. Let me take you to another world. Let's forget about this alcohol thing and go for a walk. It's darker; fewer people will be out at this time. Fresh air will help us call our reason."

He put on his jacket and sunglasses. Aylin didn't say anything. They walked down the stairs in silence. He softly grabbed her hand and said he wanted to go to Holland Park.

"Let's see if we're lucky enough to see a few stars. The weather isn't that bad today. This is what I do when I have many things bothering my soul. I open up to nature. I venture through leaves like wind. There are things you might experience simply by trying to be something else—a bird, for instance. If you try hard enough and let your feelings reach the birds, you might also feel their freedom in the skies. It's my type of meditation. You don't need to be in any particular position like the ordinary spiritual classes. You just need to believe in nature, in who you are. You'll feel a powerful energy invading your body. Relief. The reactions may differ. You might smile and you might cry, but on the way back home, there will always be a feeling of peace and rest."

"You're crazy."

"I heard a story one day. A guy lost a wheel while driving his car. It just came off. Luckily, it wasn't a busy street, and his car hit the sidewalk next to a mental hospital. The car didn't have any damage. There was a patient in a blue outfit leaning on the other side of the fence and a few other people walking around. The driver checked his car; and everything was fine, but he couldn't change the wheel by himself because he'd lost all the wheel bolts. He checked inside the car but couldn't find any. He started calling friends and people who might help. "I can't move my ass from here. I'm stuck. I have a spare wheel but no bolts. I'm screwed. I need to get there as soon as possible." The guy was screaming, losing his patience, swearing, and kicking stones on the ground.

"The patient was still there, watching the unlucky man going crazy. He felt pity for him and finally decided to speak. 'Hey! Excuse me!' the patient said.

"The guy didn't answer straight away. He thought, *Please not now. I've already had enough.*

"'Why don't you unscrew one bolt from each of the other wheels and then fix your fourth one? I'm sure you'll have a safe journey with only three bolts on each wheel. At least until you get to the closest place where you can buy some.'

"It was very hot. The driver had his head between his hands. When he heard the patient speak, he raised his head with surprise and looked at him quizzically. 'That's genius! What the hell do you do in that hospital?'

"'Well! It's people like you who made us come here. I made everyone believe I was a fool to join the house of wisdom. This place is peaceful. And we always hear and see the normal things that you people think are unusual. The drugs are also amazing and free. Have a safe journey.' He left."

Aylin laughed.

"Interesting story about you fools."

"He was right. What makes life more interesting is the unusual behaviors we see, the unusual thoughts we hear. We haven't tried to understand those people. They have a different perception of life. We must listen to them and accept the way they are. They must be free. I'm a fool, yes. Let's sit down here. This bench is nice," Lewis added.

"All right. I'm a listener today."

"No, you're here to talk as well. You can be weird too. It's your right. Think about things you normally don't think about, or when you say things you think are not wise or good enough to be told. Grab your freedom by its hands and drag it on with you. Don't wait for it to come. If you cannot be free here, you'll never be free anywhere."

"Hi guys! I hope you're having a wonderful time underneath my sky." A random guy had appeared. "I won't tell you stories. I'm a beggar. But I would have to say that you've got a wonderful woman next to you, sir. The only company I have is my bottle of wine. Unfortunately, I'm running out, and my night will be very long without it."

He hadn't finish talking when Lewis had already taken five quid out of his pocket. "I won't let you be alone. I like your honesty. Do you want a cigarette as well?"

"Yes, why not? Sweet!" With an expression of contentment on his face, he said, "Life would be much easier if everyone was like you, sir." He lit his cigarette, took a few puffs and smiled.

"Why are you outside?" Aylin asked.

"This is my home. I'm exactly like my dad. When I was born, I came out of his balls. I'm a cock. I stink of cum. I'm always hard, and I've been everywhere—entered places even when I wasn't invited. I always forgot my hat. I made a few babies. Their mothers took all my money. Life has taken everything I have from me, but it's okay. As long as I can buy some wine, I'm happy. I manage to survive; God is with me. I miss having a beautiful company like yours, dear sir! What's your name, if I may ask?"

"Of course. I'm Lewis, and this is Aylin. She's my best friend."

"I don't believe that. I can see it in her eyes. Your eyes don't hide anything either. Nothing can be this romantic. I wish I could break the barrier of that friendship you have. You both look amazing together. Just be careful, though, I was under that same impression one day. It was my last day. I actually don't know whether I live or not. Every day is the same for me, the day I met her. I got hurt, but I loved the way it happened. Who gives a shit about me? No one, not even her. But I still picture myself there on the same bench, years ago. I haven't left this place since."

"Everyone has his own story, and we all have a path to follow," Lewis answered. Lewis tried to change the subject because the old man had targeted a very sensitive one. Aylin didn't say a word, but he could hear her heartbeat. "Another cigarette?"

"Yes, but I'll have it later. I need to run before the shops close."

"Oh, sure. It's been a pleasure. You're a brave man," Lewis added.

"You're a fucking nice man. Thank you. Beautiful lady, enjoy your time in my garden. This guy has a white heart."

"I know," she said. "That's why he's my best friend. And thank you."

The beggar wrapped himself in his dirty coat and made his way to God knew where. Lewis looked at Aylin and smiled. "I liked that guy. See? How can we complain?"

"He must have endured some hard times. Poor man," Aylin said.

"No, he's not poor. He's understood the harshness of life. He's accepted it and is living happily with it. For him, life has a meaning: drinking alcohol and living reality as it is meant to be. He's the richest. He lives life as a human being. He has no ego. Well, maybe he's been stupid and silly at some point, but he's learned his lesson. He has no guilt; he has no regret. He's full of love. He loves who he is. I could perceive that."

"Lewis, don't be so blind. He's living a miserable life."

"In which sense? The cavemen were living like that. Does that mean all men were miserable, that everyone was sad?"

"Time has changed. There are some standards that we need in order to find some happiness."

"Those standards are the cause of our sadness, not the basis of our happiness. We created something to please us, we got used to it, and then when we don't have it, we mourn like hungry dogs. They're paying billions to watch the stars; this brave guy has nothing to eat. Do you think he gives a shit about whether life on Mars is possible? We're the weapons of our own destruction. The human race a clever animal? What a joke! Anyway, this guy has made my day."

He paused for a bit and then added, "Well, listen, I need to get going. Go home and rest; you need it."

"What about you?"

"I'll go home as well. I have loads of things to do."

"Okay, but we haven't finished our conversation yet. Anyway, make sure you're going home. And call me tomorrow."

"I'm sorry, I just remembered. But don't worry. I guess we'll have plenty of time to talk about everything. I'll call you. And thank you again for everything."

"Don't be silly. Any time."

Rushing to say goodbye, Lewis held Aylin in his arms and gave her a kiss on the forehead. He turned around and made his way through the long park. Lights shone everywhere. The beauty of the night had calmed down his anger. His heart felt small and cold. He could distinguish the feeling that invaded his body. He sat down on a bench and let his tears run down to get rid of his loneliness. He breathed deeply when Sweetie came back to his mind, and he prayed for whatever God he believed in to release him from that bottomless darkness.

His phone rang, but he didn't answer. He didn't even check to see who it was. He closed his eyes, and Aylin appeared in front of him. *No, no. Not Aylin, please!*

He tried to answer the question, but he couldn't. On his way to the tube station, his phone rang again and again. Ben was calling.

"Hey, Ben."

"What the fuck? I've been calling you for the last hour."

"I didn't know it was you. I didn't feel like answering."

"Aylin again?"

"No, I had some serious drama. Anyway, not important. What are you up to?"

"I was thinking about going to a strip club," Ben said.

"Oh, good. I can't say no to that."

"Meet me by the entrance in fifteen minutes."

"In twenty-five minutes. I'm quite far away."

"All right."

Lewis hung up and switched off his phone. He made up his mind and decided to join him. Instead of taking the tube, he decided to walk because it wasn't that far anyway. It started raining a little bit, which he didn't mind. Every drop that landed on his body was a call of all those girls he'd had in his bed, so cold and angry. He felt their anxiety and sense of revenge. The lights on the street were so colorful and beautifully organized to give it a lively feeling. People would rather stay outdoors than spend time at home. *Staying at home is a waste of time. It's like pretending to live. Watching movies is for those who keep dreaming of a different life; they tend to play different roles in different films. They cry when they see a love story because they wish it could happen to them. They feel sad, then happy, for an unfortunate role because it doesn't happen to them in that way. They find comfort, they pursue dreams, and they find hope. It's so boring to be behind a TV. It may be good to watch the news from time to time, but people should get to know new things about themselves first. Overall, watching TV at home is a means to escape the truth of our daily lives. I have my own role here to play, and I face it in different circumstances. I experience the secrets of the Earth no matter what the result is. I'm meant to live, not to watch TV. I just wish there was no such thing.*

Lewis's head was messed up with thoughts he didn't mean to think about. Every day was a debate, like a courtroom he couldn't leave. He was the guilty, the victim, and the judge.

Home! A movie! His thoughts were suddenly disturbed by a whistle. He realized that someone was calling him. He looked in the direction he'd heard the whistle from and saw Ben waving with his broken left hand. He'd broken it when he was a kid, but it hadn't healed properly and was curved like a crescent. Lewis could also recognize his big smile that took over half his face. He had thick lips and a front tooth that came out like an offside football player. Lewis could also perceive Ben's shiny green eyes that had turned reddish because of herbal smokes. He wore a dark suit and a striped shirt, the way Lewis always advised him to do. At first impression, people thought Ben was a drug dealer, and nobody liked him at first sight. This was how hypocritical everyone was. No one had given Ben a chance to get to know what was hidden behind that appearance. Lewis had, and the guy had become more important than anyone else. His heart was the size of his body, and that feeling gave him the look of an angel. He liked to dance in nightclubs, to drink, and to smoke the Moroccan hash always available in his wallet.

"Hey! Where the fuck have you been? What drama?"

"Sweet is dead. She killed herself."

"What?"

"You heard. Let's have a joint first. I'll tell you more."

They sat down underneath a small bridge, rolled a big spliff, and passed it around to give it more pleasure. Deep in his words, Lewis tried not to go through all the details to make the event a news article. Ben opened his mouth but didn't comment; he understood the consequences the incident might have had on Lewis.

"What about Aylin?"

"I was with her and didn't tell her anything. She shouldn't know."

"What are you going to do with her anyway? You know she loves you."

"Hey, dude! Am I really a man to love? If you knew a person you care about, would you allow her to be with me? I'm an idiot. I fuck every girl I meet. I'm an alcoholic and take drugs whenever I get the chance. Do you really want me to be with Aylin? What for? In order to mess up her life as well? No, please, not Aylin. And never mention her again."

"All right. What about your feelings toward her?"

"Yes, I love Aylin. But I can't accept seeing her suffer. Not her." Lewis threw away the end of the joint. He blew the smoke into the air and watched it disappear the way life ended for everyone on Earth. *You live a moment without knowing whether you'll be lucky enough to live throughout the whole day.* "Hey! Let's do this while we're alive. Are you ready?" Lewis said.

"I'm always ready when I'm with you, man. Fuck the whole world."

There was no doubt Lewis always felt good when he was with Ben. His best moments of laughter were when he was with him. He felt lonely without Ben's hilarious face. They got inside the club through a long corridor. The lights blinded their eyes. Ben put his hands in the air and jumped inside with his weird dance moves. The club was full, girls danced in every corner, and men swallowed their saliva.

They got a table, sat down, and lit their cigarettes. It was the only place where people could still smoke inside. Lewis had a different behavior, which was easily noticed by Ben. He invited him to dance, but Lewis rejected. "Not now," he said.

They drank shots all night, and only the bill could tell how many. Ben threw himself in the air, got a few girls to give him lap dances, and exchanged numbers with some hot ones. Lewis watched him from his chair and smiled, trying to give the impression of having fun.

All right. I'm all right, his mind said. He looked at the place the way he'd never looked at it before. *This world is absurd,* he thought. Lights, colors, pairs of boobs, alcohol, and drugs. He remained in his seat even after a few lines. Girls came to talk to him, but he didn't want to interact. He felt cold and unpleasant.

"Lewis, what the fuck? What's wrong with you?"

"Nothing. This is the way I want to enjoy tonight."

"Well, I'm not enjoying it that way."

They laughed together, and Lewis stood up. A hot girl, yes. He'd seen someone he liked. No one knew what he did. It didn't take him more than two minutes to get the girl to dance with him.

No matter how much he drank, he was always able to stand up and give a show with his moves on the dance floor. The girl rubbed her ass against him, a purely sexual dance in a purely sexual place. The smoke of cigarettes had covered the whole area, and it was very hard to see who was next to whom. Some girls were sucking cocks, and others were close to being raped by horny boys. It was a crazy night where alcohol was never an issue. Girls were a means of entertainment, but the drugs were the awakening of true selves. No one could guess what he took and how much. He sat down again on his seat, his head hanging in the air like it didn't belong to his body. The girl pushed him to lean back properly. She opened his zip and took out his penis. She put it in her mouth and started sucking it. Ben was still dancing but didn't miss the whole scene. He was always better at relating the stories experienced in different circumstances.

Lewis was there. A blowjob, drunk, high ... Fuck, it's Lewis. Ben startled. Too fast on his way to the people fighting everywhere, Ben missed a step and fell hard on one of the guys who was already lying on the floor. He felt someone grabbing his hand, then two, moving him toward the exit. Security was all over the place. Right after him, Lewis was brought outside as well. He walked calmly without trying to resist. He knew he was out anyway, and he couldn't do anything against those security monsters, as opposed to Ben, who got hit a couple of time because he was shaking uncontrollably. Ben calmed down as soon as he saw that Lewis was safe and clean. Lewis walked toward Ben and smiled.

"What the hell happened to you?" Lewis asked.

"I don't know. I saw you fighting, but I fell on my way to you. I fell on someone's back. I put my elbows forward to protect my face, and when I hit the guy, I heard him scream like a dog. But what happened? Did they attack you?"

"Just forget it."

"What do you mean? We were having fun. And how come you're acting so sober?"

"I woke up in the middle of a nightmare, and I realized it was reality. When I saw the girl blowing my cock, I flipped and slapped her in the face, and she fell over. A part of me rejected it as if I had someone else inside my body that helped my hand push away that girl."

"No! I don't know which part of the bullshit you just told me is your nightmare. I hope not the blowjob."

"Someone's hell can be someone else's heaven, and vice versa."

"I don't get it. What's wrong with you, man? Something must have happened if you're talking about your heart and someone inside of you. This Aylin girl is fucking you up."

"Don't fucking annoy me, and again, stop mentioning her name, please. I'm just not in the mood. Maybe I've had enough."

Is it Aylin? Lewis kept repeating in his head. He tried to ignore the idea. The girl was untouchable. *Aylin! No, never. Oh, Aylin, if only ...* His thoughts battled against his heart while Ben related to him what had happened inside the club.

"Hey!" Ben shouted. "Are you even listening to me?"

"Oh, yes, bro. Sorry, I don't know what's wrong with me. I don't feel well. Let's go to my place. Really, I'm done with this shit."

The journey home was very quick. They opened a bottle of Chivas and drank it all. Lewis laughed at every word Ben uttered—jokes about Indians, the French, and mostly Algerians. They both got drunk and fell asleep on the sofa.

Ben had already left when Lewis woke up. He got into his bed and slept longer. Aylin called his phone many times, but he couldn't hear his phone ring.

Someone was vigorously knocking on the door. He looked through the peephole. It wasn't Aylin. He went back to his bed. He grabbed his phone and called her back.

"You asshole. Where have you been? I told you to text me when you get home."

"Good morning."

"Fuck you! It's 6:00 p.m."

"For me, the morning doesn't have the same significance as you normal people define it. For me, the morning is not the first hours of the sunrise. For me, it's simple: any time I wake up is morning, and any time I spend outside is my day, whether it's light or dark. Sorry. I went out with Ben yesterday."

"You see. You said you were going home. You cannot change."

"Well, I ended up coming home. I haven't slept with any random girl this time. It's already a big thing."

"I'm surprised, retard."

"I'm tired of everything. I'll take it easy from now on."

"You'd better. And start by finding a new job."

"Sure, will do. Be safe. I'll speak to you soon."

Things got mixed up in his head. In fact, he needed a job, otherwise he wouldn't be able to survive. He needed to be able to pay for his drinks, some drugs, his rent, and his food. That cost lot of money. *Fuck money!* He smiled as he remembered his friend.

"We need to find a job where we earn lot of money and have no need to work," he'd said once.

"Ha-ha! And what kind of job would that be?"

"This is the question I'm asking you to answer. Let me know once you've found it."

Crazy lad, he thought. *If only we didn't have to bother too much about work, life would be so much easier. The old times again. Man was a hunter. Yes, we were hunters. Life has no meaning anymore because we've stopped hunting.*

He really needed a job. He opened his laptop and tried to apply for some vacancies. Nothing was interesting. He didn't know what to do. He could be anything and could work anywhere. Because he had lot of options, it became harder to apply for any. Accountancy, finance, management, languages ... He started the first application, got bored, and closed his laptop with a lack of ambition.

He lacked ambition because he lacked faith. He lacked faith because his life was empty. He didn't believe in anyone, not even in himself. He'd drowned his life with his own hands. *What for? Whom for?* All those efforts to afford a better life, all those sacrifices for a soul that didn't exist in his body—or rather, had died at some point during the course of his life. Something or somebody had taken it. *I need to have faith in something. Faith is anything that gives life a purpose. The thing that drives you to live for it, a reason.* He decided to wait for the seed to come, to be planted in the garden of his hopes. A dead garden needed life that would surface to give meaning to the everyday mornings and nights. But how long would he have to wait? He didn't know, and neither did he speculate. Nobody could predict. He hated predictions and never believed in superstitions. He had five senses, and only those counted.

He walked out with a cigarette in his hand, dragged his body and mind outside, and ventured around common roads he regularly walked. They seemed different every time, although physically nothing ever changed.

His mind was modeling the roads, the streets, and the people crossing his way. He also undressed every girl he looked at. That was his world, the only common thing he shared with every man. He sat down on a bench and smoked a joint. Then he felt a bit better. He stepped on his heart to strangle his feelings and headed to central London. He felt lonely. He went on Facebook and wrote one message, which he sent to different girls: "Hi, baby. Long time no see! I was away for a couple of weeks. Just came back. What are you doing tonight? We could meet up for a drink. Let me know."

He had a few drinks and tried to talk to a few girls by the bar. He danced a little bit and came out for more cigarettes. He kept checking Facebook, but no one answered. He felt horny. He smiled and remembered his friend Kyle.

"Man, come out with me. The world is out there. You complain of being alone, but you never try. There are so many girls you could meet up with. Come and have fun," Lewis told Kyle.

"Lewis, we have different philosophies of life. I like it simple. It's true that we all need someone—this feeling of love, affection, and comfort. But for the time being, I'm more than happy by myself. When it comes to sex, I try to avoid all that process of trying too hard to talk to someone, which is usually like an exam to me, and then inviting her for a drink and spending all my money. All of this to wonder whether she'll end up in my bed. For me, as opposed to you, it's always more likely not going to happen. If I want to have sex, I pay a girl. I do whatever I want with her, I calm down my desires, and I go sleep. It's cheaper, and I put less effort in it. As long as I have the money to pay, I believe there is nothing better than a prostitute. She knows she's working. You can have a conversation, and it's up to you where the limit is. She doesn't ask you questions you won't like."

"Well, in any case, a woman is like a gambling machine, you spend all your money and you win nothing."

Lewis left the bar and decided to go to a whore place in Soho for the first time in his life. He never thought he'd do it, but he felt the need to savor the moment. The street was busy, and bars were everywhere. People were outside smoking, drinking, and walking in every direction. Lights were so bright that a drunkard could hardly distinguish between daylight and nighttime. He got to the place and looked at it from the outside. It was colored red, with small windows upstairs where he could see an obscure light. Curtains were half open and music was on. He found it hard to get in through all the people surrounding the place. He felt weird and ashamed. *Paying for sex is a sin.* He'd never sinned that way. He took a deep breath and walked in quickly. Very narrow stairs took him to the first floor. One door on the left and another one on the right. He knocked on both.

A girl from the left door opened. "Hey! Welcome."

Oh, God, he thought.

"Come in, please. You'll have to wait a little bit; she's busy," she carried on.

"Oh, sure." He sighed with relief.

He realized she was a kind of receptionist. He got into a small living room with two small sofas, a microwave, and a TV. There were two books on the shelf, three glasses on the table, and a tip tray.

"Sit down and feel comfortable. She'll come shortly," she said.

"Is she hot?"

"She's nice, a beautiful Russian."

I know what that's like. Russians—blonde, tall. They can be beautiful or ugly, and there's nothing in between, but they're usually good in bed.

He sat down, trying to imagine the scene. But this kind of situation was nonexistent in his mind. He'd never experienced that before.

"What do you want to do?" she asked.

"Watch a movie! What else do you expect me to do here? What's on the menu?"

Before he'd finished his sentence, they heard a knock on the door. They both looked at the entrance, and the door was opening. Lewis's heartbeat increased in speed. *Yes, I'll fuck for money, but she has to be hot! Oh, God, what am I doing here?*

Someone came in, and the tension made the scene last longer as the door opened slowly. Blonde, tall, skinny, fat, ugly, pimples—she could be anything!

"Hi!" the person said once completely visible.

"Hi," the receptionist said. "How are you? Take a seat please."

"I'm good, thank you."

Lewis put his head between his hands and tried not to react. His patience had almost reached its limits. A waiting room with a fat Arab guy was the last thing he'd expected.

Calm down. You wanted to experience this. You wanted to know what it's like, what it feels like.

An Arab guy! The man's face was pale and full of pimples. He had a bag on his left shoulder and a long black coat. His breath was heavy; the stairs were too much for him. His body sweated as if he'd just finished a gym session. He sat down on a chair twice smaller than his ass and started checking his phone without saying a word.

The most dangerous and common sexual frustration in the whole world is the Arab one. It's annoying, actually. These guys don't choose their faith. Society has made their lives more difficult. It became cultural. These men cannot utter a word in front of a girl, even where women are the ones to make the first step. They don't have the right to do so, and they've never known the language of women. The whole story reminded him of Algeria and the Arab culture. What a curse I ran away from.

"Hey! Are you coming or what?" a female voice came to his ear, cutting him off from his world of debates and bringing him back to the world of reality.

Lewis looked at her in surprise and stood up. A quick reaction to sex. *Sexy.*

"Follow me."

He followed her footsteps while watching her white slim body. She wore reddish underwear and ten-inch heels. He didn't know how many steps they mounted. He got to her room before he knew it. Everything was tidy and clean. There were a few candles lit, and a scent of chamomile spread all over the room. There was a TV on a small table in the corner, discreet music playing in the background and flashing lights by the opposite window. She opened the drawer of the nightstand and took out a condom. She looked beautiful, and he wished he'd met her somewhere else. She leaned back, spread her legs, and applied lubricant on her pussy. Lewis used the protection, looked at her, and paused.

"I don't want to fuck," he said.

"Sorry?"

"I'm speaking English. I don't want to fuck. Give me a blowjob."

He sat down on the edge of the bed with his trousers down to his knees. Her nails were shiny and long. She had a piercing on her tongue that he could feel every time she licked the head of his cock. *Quite exciting.* He felt his body shivering from head to toe, an electrical current that created a short circuit in his balls. Like a volcanic eruption, his condom filled up with cum. He let go of his body, falling backward on the bed, and took a few minutes to savor the orgasmic feeling. She certainly was good. She said something that he couldn't hear. She gave him wet tissues and asked him to get dressed.

"Why didn't you want to have proper sex?"

"It wouldn't be something I would call proper sex. Besides, I don't like to see legs open like Ali Baba's cave. There's a lot missing here for the act to be called proper sex."

"Show me that next time."

"I'm afraid there won't be a next time." He grabbed his jacket and left.

Sex ... Is this really what they call sex? Poor creatures. What about the girl? My heart hurts. What about all those moments you enjoy spending with a girl, eating, drinking, flirting, getting into bed, taking your time? Run over someone's body, then have sex, make love, hug afterward, kiss, and fall asleep entangled together? They're nonexistent there. We surely can pay to penetrate a vagina, but we can never pay to get some affection, a feeling you share while exchanging this extraordinary experience of making love. Money cannot pay for the supreme orgasm. Money! Money! Sex! I'm losing it.

He didn't see anybody on the street. It was dark in his world. He discovered two new feelings that raised his pitiful heart to an unknown level. *The girl in need of money uses her body. The man in need of sex uses his money. It's never enough, a process that will never stop. Those feelings engendered new ones; anger and guilt are the major ones. Frustration, sex, and money have led society to commit crimes against itself. No one should be paying for sex!*

He scratched his head and his chin and tried to forget about it.

Chapter 7

"For some, love is the life of their dreams, and for
others, the life of their dreams is pleasure."

"Ben! Where are you?" Lewis said, calling him on the phone.

"You don't know what happened today," Ben said.

"Tell me."

"It's my flatmate, the Pakistani girl. She fucked up."

"What did she do?" Lewis was laughing already.

"I woke up this morning. I was thirsty, so I went straight to the kitchen to have some water. I saw the girl like a Jackie Chan by the sink. She was washing her feet in there."

Lewis laughed.

"You can laugh as much as you want. I couldn't believe it. I pinched my skin to wake up; I thought I was having a nightmare. I rubbed my eyes thoroughly, but it still looked real. She was actually washing her feet inside the sink in the kitchen. *In the kitchen.* Knowing how short she is, I couldn't even figure out how she managed to get her feet there. She was stretched like a frog. When I asked her what she was doing, she said the bathroom was busy."

"Ha-ha! You should have told her to shower there next time."

"I can't deal with this shit anymore. I'm moving out. Fucking dirty asses. You know I need to win the lottery."

"Ha-ha, sure, you should."

"I'll buy a luxurious nightclub. I'll drink alcohol every night, take every drug, and fuck whores until I die the happiest death."

"I don't think that would be called a happy life, though. I'm already tired of this shit."

"Come to my place and have a joint with me, and I'm sure you'll change your mind," Ben said.

"Nah. I'm going back home. I'm not drinking tonight. I'm cutting down on everything."

"There's something wrong with you, and you're not telling me."

"What's wrong and what isn't?"

"It's wrong when you have a life and then change it."

"Nothing is wrong with both. There's absolutely nothing wrong with changing your life. I've enjoyed my life so much since I got here. Never felt so free. If I had to do it again, I'd do it exactly the same way. I wouldn't change anything, even the times I've been punched in the face, even the times I cried under the rain. It wouldn't be as exciting without those bad moments. They make me laugh now. The beauty of the bad and good moments I had is part of my lifestyle, and every lifestyle has its own beauty. You need change to experience all of it."

"There are a few things I'd have changed, actually," Ben said.

"What are they?"

"If I were you, I'd have quickly married one of those girls to sort out my papers here."

"It's not that easy, Ben. I know there are many girls in my life. Although my visa will expire soon, I still think I can find the woman I want to marry, not the one I have to."

"I think the best is to find someone I can pay to help me with my papers. In that case, I wouldn't have to jail myself in a relationship, and I'd still have this much fun, probably staying single forever."

"That's not the ideal world either. I'm contemplating to stop this make-believe thing. We live once, and we try not to regret what we do, but it's better if you have nothing to regret at all. If you follow the right path, then one life is more than enough."

"I agree, but you never get to choose how to make it. Things happen."

"Sometimes, if not most of the time, you don't choose. But whatever happens, you should make the best of it. It's time to stop dreaming and to start living a dream. Your dream can be anything, not necessarily your own Canary Island or a hot Jacuzzi with ten sexy birds. A dream can be early morning sunshine. It could be a smile; it could be someone's company.

Your dream resides within you and around you. It's up to you to free it and walk with it hand in hand."

"Lewis, you talk like an old woman. Stop this bullshit. My dream is to win the lottery. Sunshine, my ass. I've lived all my life under the sun. I got tanned, nothing else."

"You should dare to face the truth. Every sentence you say is your last. You can never go back in time."

"I've always tried to find my own reality, but I never managed."

"Ben, if you're trying, there's a chance you get to know other realities or live other lives, but it will never be enough. You have to believe in it. While you're trying to get something, you should never forget to realize that what you've acquired or lived until now is very precious. In that case, you enjoy living your life with what you've got, and you have the hope to get a better one. Someone who believes in success is always full of hope, energy, and happiness. Think about that for a while."

"You might be right. But this discussion makes me want to throw up."

"You know, life has given me a new challenge. Are there two new, different paths to follow? The path of love or the path of ego. Both could be paths to hell, and both could be paths to heaven. I know both can't be the same. The challenge is to choose. On either path, there's the option of giving up, and there are the companions of sacrifice—in other words, sadness and regret. On either path, there's partial happiness. There's love or the desire to devour life just as it comes. For some, love is the life of their dreams, and for others, the life of their dreams is pleasure. I may not agree, although sometimes I get confused. In this case, both are different. Therefore, my challenge starts now. Never let your love go. Struggle for the life of your dreams in the here and now."

"Oh, man, you have a problem, and it seems to bother me as well. It reminds me of those times when you were in love."

"Love has never left my heart. Love isn't something you get from someone. It's not a common feeling you share. It's rather something you give. I've always given my heart to everyone around me. It's just that it takes more to be an exception, to be the right person or complete love."

"This conversation would be more interesting if we were having a joint. I also have a bottle of whiskey."

"No, man. I'd love to, but I'll skip this time. I might come to see you tomorrow."

"All right. Take care."

"Thanks, you too."

It started raining again. It was August. Everyone around was pissed off and complaining. *We've never had a summer in this shit country.* He walked through a beautiful, colorful park that was almost empty because of the rain. He perceived an old man standing in the middle. Lewis thought he'd do the same. He decided to get close and try to share that moment of pleasure with the strange man. The rain was soft and the grass was wet. The temperature wasn't very low. It was a little windy, but he didn't care. The old man was steady, staring at the sky with his hands in his pockets. It would look very weird to a normal personal. Who did that? He looked alive, just standing there. He'd applied black eyeliner that ran all over his face like tears because of the rain. Both his eyes were closed, and he breathed so slowly that it was hardly noticeable. There was nobody around. He didn't have anything on him. His clothes seemed pretty clean but damp; he certainly wasn't a homeless person. What was he doing there?

Lewis loved the rain. Many times he'd walked long distances underneath the drizzling skies. He stood in front of the old man, closed his eyes, and directed his face toward the sky. Rain fell heavily. The feeling was phenomenal. He felt the man in front of him moving. He walked closer to Lewis, who made a sudden, involuntary, cautious movement.

"Don't worry," the man said with a hoarse voice. *A whiskey drinker,* Lewis thought. "Apply this on your eyes. I never cry; my eyes are dry. But when I apply this and stay underneath the rain, I feel like I'm crying. Tears relieve our bodies from pain, sorrow, and sadness. Do you cry?"

"Yes, sometimes, when I get too emotional."

"That's good. Some men cannot reveal their weaknesses to save their manliness. Hiding your tears is like hiding your heart. It's who you are. So let it be."

"How come you've never cried?" Lewis asked.

"I've been through a lot of pain, increasing gradually, an everyday feeling. I got used to it. I can be emotional, down deep, but my eyes never secrete any water. I don't know why, though. This is why I'm here. This exercise helps me recover from my usual discomfort."

"All right, let's try it. I already know the secret of tears, but not with eyeliner or this way, under the rain."

"Give your spirit a break; let it go for a few minutes. Feel the water on your face. The black liner will give you a miserable face, and your heart will feel the comfort of your well-being. Stop thinking. It sounds almost impossible, right? If you've ever liked challenges, this is it."

"All right."

Lewis applied the eyeliner, put his hands inside his jeans' pockets, and stood, his legs shoulder width apart. Then he directed his face toward the sky. He was already wet by the time he got there. The rain was stronger than it had been before. He didn't feel cold; the temperature was perfect. Images of everything crossed his mind. Trying not to think was not an easy task for him. Images—the things that bothered him a lot every morning once he opened his eyes. He saw things he wished he'd had seen, although he never got irritated by their lack. He had a wish. Not caring was just a lie at the end of the day. While trying to stop thinking, he started thinking deeper than he should have. He tried to concentrate on the rain itself; that was the key. Every drop on his face was a blessing, a natural massage that gave a different feeling.

He was carried on a boat in an endless sea. The more he thought, the higher the waves grew. He came out of his thoughts and looked at himself from another angle. He was the audience of his own movie. He observed his thoughts and wisely started looking at his confusions one by one. The clearer he came to a conclusion, the calmer the water got. He stopped moving, leaning down on a flat raft. The world was smooth and calm. The rain was still falling down, two people facing each other in a middle of a park. When Lewis felt he was already there for too long, he decided to open his eyes. He saw a blurry gray sky as the rain blinded his eyes.

Lewis realized the man was no longer in front of him. He wanted to thank him for the moment, a lovely spiritual practice. His clothes were all wet, his legs were dirty, and home was quite far away. He walked toward the exit to leave the place, but he heard a sudden whistle coming from the tall trees. The old man was there; Lewis recognized his strange cloak. The guy was waving, which could mean only one thing: he was calling him.

The adventure has not finished yet, I guess, Lewis thought. *This guy is interesting. I wonder what he's got on his mind this time?* "Hi, sir! What's your name?" Lewis asked.

"My name's not that important to be known."

"If you say so. I thought you'd left. I wanted to thank you for the meditation. It was relaxing."

"I didn't invite you; you came by yourself. I believe you found a few answers up there."

"The problem is I've always known those answers. I simply never knew how to organize them in my life. Maybe I need to do it more often. What I realized is this exercise can never make you cry. Unless your heart is deeply hurt and you're emotionally sensitive, tears will never come!"

"Your soul cries instead."

"How come you've never cried before? It's very hard to believe. I'm still concerned by this idea."

"I don't have a switch for tears."

Lewis asked, "Have you ever been in love?"

"You're asking too many questions. You can go."

"I'm sorry. Maybe because you helped me find comfort, I thought I might be able to draw a tear from your eyes."

"I told you to go away. Come back next time. I'm here every time it rains around this time of the day."

"As you wish. Once again, thank you."

Lewis was thrilled by his reaction to the question. The most fundamentals, the basics of a human's comfort in nature, shelter, food, and a woman we love—he probably didn't have any of these. It left him wandering around in parks and living in an imaginary world. How could he not be able to cry? Or had he cried so much that he couldn't do it anymore?

Lewis made his way back, reviewing the whole scene. He wondered whether that guy existed only in that current life. What would be the meaning of life in the man's own world? What he saw was just part of his destiny, of Lewis's own realm. Was it a challenge to see that guy crying? Why would he? *We cannot stop things from happening. Otherwise, life would turn out differently, and the difference could be worse than it already is.*

The little pleasure was transformed into a little sneeze, pain after joy. His cigarettes were all wet; he couldn't light that marvelous killer.

Luckily, he had some in his wardrobe; he simply needed to be patient until he got home. He sat down by the stairs and gave himself the satisfaction of smoking a long joint. He felt high and didn't think about anything. His skin was shivering, so he got rid of his clothes and walked into the bathroom. *Hot water!* He decided to stay at home. He needed to have a private session with himself.

He texted Aylin.

"Hi, I'm at home. I'll be staying in for the next two or three days. I need to fill out some applications. So if you don't hear anything from me, just remember I'm in a safe place. I also have things on mind I need to sort out. I hope you're okay. Take care."

He switched off his phone and made a cup of hot tea for a change. The taste of lemon was refreshing to his mind. The ideal world! The ideal girl—who could it be? He couldn't tell. Nobody could tell. That guy in the park wasn't crying; he never cried, and he probably hadn't yet met anyone for whom he could cry. His feelings were dormant. *He needs someone to wake them up,* Lewis thought. He checked the weather forecast and smiled. Raining all day the next day. It wasn't very surprising; the climate was almost always the same throughout the whole year. But Lewis didn't want to miss seeing that guy again. He jumped onto his bed, covered himself, and fell asleep as soon as his head touched the pillow. He felt a bit weak because of the cold he'd caught.

Cold it was again at the same place and same time in the wide park. A few things were different, but he couldn't tell which. This time, the man was in a suit, a red tie, and a white shirt. Lewis opened his mouth when he saw tears on the man's face. The man he didn't know the name of, the man he didn't know anything about. All he knew was the guy had never cried before, and this wasn't the case anymore. He couldn't hide his face. His hands were stuck inside his pockets. There was no eyeliner on his face. Lewis could see tears falling down his cheeks. He didn't know what to do.

"Sir, I don't know if I'm to be happy for you because it's an achievement, or to feel pity because you're actually crying. Enjoy the expression of real tears," Lewis said.

He looked like he was crying for the first time in his life. He couldn't hear the world around him. His mouth was wide open, and his eyes were tightly closed. Lewis watched him for a while; he wanted to allow him to cry in order to ease his pain. His tears couldn't stop streaming all over his face.

Lewis made a move forward and put his hand on the man's shoulder. "What made you cry so much, sir? I'm thrilled."

"I'm feeling," he replied. "I'm feeling ..."

"What are you feeling?"

"I'm feeling pity. I'm feeling sad. I'm feeling torn."

"But why? It's normal, so don't worry. Everything is going to be fine."

"I'm fine, and I always will be fine. It's not about me—it's about you. I'm crying for you."

Lewis's heart jumped in his chest when he heard the man's words. He stood still and fixed the guy with a stare. "And why would you cry for me?" Lewis asked with astonishment.

"You're dead. You're dead; leave the girl alone. Let her be. She's innocent. You're dead."

The old man opened his eyes, grabbed Lewis by his arm, and pulled a knife from behind his back. He spread his lips, showed his teeth, and screamed, "I have to kill you!"

In the dark night, Lewis opened his eyes on his bed. His breath was heavy, his throat was thirsty, and his body was sweaty. He got up, drank some water, and lay down on the pillow. He lit a cigarette. *What does he mean by "You're dead. Leave her alone"?* He couldn't go back to sleep. The world had taken another alleyway in his brain. Struggling between reality and dreams, he couldn't distinguish between the two; they seemed the same. They both had happened in the past, and they both were a memory. It felt the same in different dimensions. A cigarette wasn't enough, and neither was a pack. He kept smoking.

The time came when he had to get up. The man should be there, waiting for him. He felt weird, he felt paranormal. He put on a warm jacket and left in order to find answers to his questions. He found the situation spine-tingling. He was scared. He feared so many things but didn't know what exactly. *Leave her alone? Who? Is it Aylin?*

He got to the park and walked around. There was nobody. He sat down on a bench and started crying without getting underneath any rain. He didn't need to use the eyeliner; he didn't need to stand up in the middle of nowhere. He could do it without getting a cold, without forcing it to happen. The tears were tears of hope and despair. He wanted to have answers to think about. But life had never given him the choice; he'd always had to struggle in order to attain his objectives. His emotions drove him up the wall. He wished at that point that he was like that guy. He wished he'd never cried.

A voice interrupted his thoughts. It was the old man. "Looks like you're letting out your anger?"

When Lewis heard his voice, he stopped crying and dried his tears straight away.

"It's all right; just let your tears be. That was the purpose of yesterday's session."

"I had a dream about you last night."

"I know."

"You know? How do you know?"

"I had the same dream."

"What does that mean?"

"I could read a few things on your face yesterday. I wanted you to come back, and maybe I have a message for you. I'm not sure whether I can tell you. it may change your life in a good way—or in a very bad way."

"So what is it?"

"I can see puzzlement on your face. I can see all the things you're going through. I see you have a brave heart, a sincere personality. You're a very charming person enthused by a few people. But don't let your charming face spoil your future. You can be an artist, but remember that artists always die poor and miserable. You'll have to make a choice, a sacrifice. It will happen very soon. Get ready—you might have an emotional breakdown. And most important, save those you love."

"Save those I love? A sacrifice? What's that all about?"

"I cannot tell you more. I was expecting you to come. You made me cry in a dream. Thank you. Your life is in your hands now; only the right decision will lead you to your extreme happiness. I must say it's a difficult path. Goodbye. God be with you."

The man disappeared in the bush. Lewis fell to his knees and cried more than he'd ever cried before. He screamed loudly and hit the ground many times with his fists, swearing and blaming himself for never having taken the right decision. Regret, confusion, yesterday, tomorrow …

Then he calmed down on the grass. He managed to get up after a while. He didn't know what time it was or how long he'd stayed there. Nothing mattered to him anymore. He sat down and lit a cigarette. Hours passed, with people coming in and out. His eyes were still closed.

"Hi, sir! Take this." The voice of a little girl came to his ears.

He looked at her and saw she was handing him a small yellowish flower. "Oh, thank you. This is sweet."

"I love flowers," she said.

"Yes, they're beautiful."

"Why are you crying, sir?"

He hadn't expected the question. "Er … I … I'm happy."

"Really? When I'm happy, I smile."

"Yes, exactly, that's good. Sometimes when we're very happy, our emotions overwhelm us. Happiness can make you cry, but you don't feel pain. Some people cry when they celebrate. Crying doesn't always mean being sad. It's complicated. You'll understand one day."

"Jenny! Come here. I told you not to talk to strangers," her mum shouted from a distance.

"Go! Run!" Lewis said.

"Mama, he's crying," she answered, running toward her.

"I always tell you not to go venture like that by yourself, next to strangers." The mother grabbed the girl's hand and pulled her aggressively. He could hear the mum's voice echoing around the place. He tried to ignore her, but a few words surfaced to his mind.

A stranger, don't venture! What kind of education is that? We're supposed to teach our kids to be adventurous; I guess this is the whole point of our lives. Daring to cross the borders gives birth to a lot of confidence. This is a wild life, and only the adventurer discovers the secrets of its land. Taking risks is what makes the course more enjoyable, and with whom do we do it? Strangers of course. The strangers are our challenge. Everyone's words, everyone's thoughts. And if a trap is meant to happen, then let it be. It shouldn't stop us from carrying on another route to accomplish our main goal, the adventure of life. What a boring kid this one will be! A modern human.

For a while, Lewis's mind wasn't preoccupied with the things on Earth. He thought about the miracle of life, of birth—the purpose in general, the creation of society, myths, and religion.

Oh, religion, he thought. *If only it was a personal and private practice, then the world would have been perfect. Death is the only reason religion exists, the boundary of our lives. The more we think about it, the more attached we are to it. It has always been this way, and as a result, some people created a common spirit. They talk about it, together they pray for it, and they believe that the spirit will give them a better place. A place that no one knows where it is or how it looks. All imaginary. It's like playing in an endless show. People take part in it until death swipes them up.*

Other people created another practice—or religion, as they call it— because they didn't like the first group's philosophy or doctrine. And now they're fighting. They're fighting for a reason that doesn't exist. Their obsession made people forget about the real adventure of life they were meant to follow. The whole thing became a practice of violence. The world is at war. Muslims kill Christians, and Christians kill Muslims. And they teach their kids to be the same. They brainwash their sons and daughters to become models of the same thinking, but never a new entity with a different outcome.

I'm done with this nonsense. When I look at people, I wonder what is the exact thing that pushes them away from life, that pushes them to always think about death and to fear death. I believe it's a weakness, it's giving up. And sometimes I think it's a choice. I don't know how you can follow that choice if it's not something cultural, traditional, brainwashing. Some tribes in Africa cut their faces and wear weird piercings for rituals that change their physical features. They paint themselves and call their spirits for one reason or another. What an amazing and at the same time silly thing to do. Maybe it's good to do it for fun, to laugh about it. It's not there; nothing is there. There is space, oxygen, and nature. There should be a lot of thoughts to be expressed, a lot of innovations to be made. Technology could be much more advanced if people hadn't wasted their time fighting for God. Reading religious books would be a nice debate to hold. But making a kid learn long chapters by heart obviously affects children's thoughts, feelings, and personality. It creates fears in their bright light, in the heart. If only they had to learn all of that as a subject to develop this world's value—the chance of being alive. I wish they'd put that much effort in investing in freeing their minds instead of restricting them. Why is it that the level of cleverness in a human being is never higher than his stupidity? How can we change this world? Well, I guess this cannot be my mission. I'd rather save myself from these foolish doctrines. My next path is in front of me. I have the power to decide whether or not I can take it. And if death stops me from doing so, then at the end of the day, I've lived as a man, and only as a man I shall die.

He realized he was back home only when he had to take out his keys to open the door. He was amazed by the power of thinking in general. Time had no meaning. He lived shorter, but he processed tons of ideas in his brain. Time ran fast, and the outside world was blank. He felt cold. He took a shower, smoked a joint, drank some whiskey, and jumped on the sofa.

He felt hungry, but he'd never liked eating. He thought that sitting down at a table was a waste of time. The truth was he found it hard to find something tasty enough to like; he'd rather not eat than eat something disgusting. He thought about going to a health shop to buy some pills to replace his meals. In fact, he left and stopped at the first shop he saw. He walked around and looked at all the different pills humans had created.

"Can I help you, sir?" a girl's voice asked.

Lewis kept his eyes focused on reading some notes on a box. When he'd finished, he turned around and was startled as his eyes met with hers. "Oh, sorry! I was lost in my thoughts. I hadn't expected anyone to talk to me."

She closed her eyes, tilted her head a bit to the side, and smiled. "It's my job. Are you looking for something particular?"

"Not really. I don't eat a lot, and I thought I might take something to help me keep up with my days."

"Sure. So you don't have an appetite?"

"Oh, no! No, I just don't like eating. I want something that replaces food, so I won't have to sit down at a table or chew some tasteless meat and vegetables."

She smiled again. This time, he looked at her closely and noticed her wide blue eyes. "Well, sir," she answered, "I'm afraid we don't have anything that replaces food, but I can recommend multivitamin pills, which can complete your daily meals. One pill a day is more than enough."

"Yes, I'll take that. Thanks for your help."

"You're welcome."

"I don't mean just the pills; I think I've found my inspiration for today."

"Excuse me?" she replied.

"Your eyes. I already know what to write about your eyes. They're amazing. I'll go to the bar next door and write it down for you."

"Oh! Really?"

"Yes, right now, before I lose it. Get the pills ready. I'll be back. Oh! Can I borrow a pen and paper?"

"Sure. Are you serious?"

"Give me fifteen minutes. Let me have a look again!"

Her reddening face didn't hide her shyness. She went behind the counter. She pulled out a pen and tore off a piece of paper from a notebook.

"Oh, can I have more page? Please."

"Sure. Actually, why don't you write it in this notebook?"

"Oh! That would be great." He grabbed the notebook, smiled with lot of affection and said, "Thank you. I will be back."

"Fifteen minutes is too short to surprise me. You'd better hurry up," she added.

Not only was it a deep inspiration that he felt, but it was also a challenge he wanted to face. For a moment, he had some doubts. He made sure his pills would be ready for his return and made his way out.

All Bar One was the pub nearest to the shop. Luckily, it was almost empty. The music was low and soft. He sat down by the bar, ordered a shot of coffee tequila, and opened the notebook to the last page. His hand slide across the notebook. The lines filled up with words, just words. He almost forgot his shot of tequila. He downed it quickly and carried on writing. He checked the time, put down his pen, and closed the notebook.

"Can I please have one more shot?"

"Sure."

He pulled out a note, put it on the tip tray together with his bill, and told the bartender to keep the change.

"Thank you, sir. Have a good evening."

"Thanks, you too."

He stood in front of the shop and wondered why he had to do this. Part of it was fun, and another part was the challenge. The challenge was not to get the girl; he'd already made up his mind to stop messing around. He entered. He looked around but didn't see the girl. At the counter, there was another girl serving customers. He waited for his turn and asked for his pills. At first he hesitated, but then he resolved to ask where the girl who had served him before was.

The cashier nicely told him that she'd had to take an early break. "She should be back in the next twenty minutes."

"All right. Could you please give her this notebook? It's hers."

"Sure, will do."

"Thank you," he said, and he left as quickly as he could.

She sat down on the floor and read the text again. She turned the pages one by one. There was no phone number, and there were no contact details. She gave it to her colleague to read. She needed to share those words with her.

"Oh, my God! Is this the guy that who earlier to pick up some pills? Who is he?"

She told her the whole story. She didn't understand what it was about. The spontaneous and funny guy hadn't left any contact details. What was the whole point, then? The words were appreciated. She wasn't sure he meant all he'd said, but it was nice to feel the attention given to her. A random guy; he was there. She had her blue eyes, and she'd never known how blue they were. She'd lived seeing them the same way every day, and then this guy came and gave them life, a better life than before.

"This is beautiful. I'm sure he'll be back," her colleague told her.

Lewis, walking on the streets of west London, didn't have the intention of going back. He'd already hurt enough girls in his life. This time, his brain was working. His heart rejected the suffering he might cause anyone. Maybe that was the beginning of a new life, changing the way he always behaved toward women. *The girl might feel happy right now.* A gift that she'd received from a random guy. Comforting words that could boost her confidence. He meant what he'd written, but that text could have been written to any girl with blue eyes. There was a lack of emotions. He probably would have done better if his heart had been involved. Who deserved to hear those words? Trying to find the answer was a waste of time.

He sat down on a wooden bench and lit a cigarette. A few minutes later, while he contemplated the beauty of the architecture around, his phone rang. It was Aylin. He had to answer.

"Hey! What's up?"

"I'm good. I just thought maybe because you're not working at the moment, and I've finished my exams, it would be a good idea if we could go on holiday somewhere to relax. Just you and me for a change."

"Sounds great. I'd love to. That's exactly what I need," Lewis said.

"Before your visa expires, we'll go to Vienna."

"Wow! A beautiful city. Aylin, just to remind you, I don't have a job. That means I might not be able to afford a luxurious trip."

"I've already booked everything. Next Friday!"

"What? Are you serious? That's in a week's time!"

"I thought the sooner, the better. And knowing how spontaneous you are, I thought you'd really appreciate it."

"I'm very surprised, and hell yes, let's do it. But you'll have to tell me how much it costs. I'll pay you back. Okay?"

"Sure. So we're going? Good news. Get your ass ready, retard."

"Ha! I'll come to your place later to see you. I'll try to! I might meet up with Ben."

"Okay, just let me know."

After he hung up, he knew that the moment of truth was approaching. That feeling scared the shit out of him. The sacrifice, love, visa expiring, the man in the park, and his dream. His head was a total mess ...

Chapter 8

"What makes a place beautiful is the people you're with."

To distract himself from the idea of the trip, Lewis called Ben, but Ben didn't respond; he was probably working. Lewis entered the first bar he found and ordered a few shots to warm himself up. He drank all evening. He couldn't stop thinking about Aylin and the purpose of her trip. He couldn't understand her goal, and he didn't want to stick to it. His predictions were very negative. He wanted to call her back and say he wouldn't be able to make it. The drinks were there, as well as a pack of cigarettes in his pocket and a piece of Moroccan hash. He felt irritated. He left the bar and walked back to the station to go home. He wanted to escape that desire of going out, that hunger for alcohol and drugs. It was a little cold, the awakening of winter.

The streets were still full of people; some were waiting for others, and some walked around in every direction. Those people were faceless; he even managed not to hear their voices. It was an empty world. What had created that effect? Was it Aylin and her trip? Was it his fear to face the truth? Was it just his lifestyle, or was it the way things were meant to be? He lowered his head and stared at the ground as he kept walking without any destination.

There was a call coming from somewhere, which happened to him quite often. It wasn't his name. He saw a shadow next to him. The shadow had a body, and the body poked him with a sweet hello reaching his ears. He stopped as he finally recognized the girl from the pills shop.

"Hey! Sorry to bother you. I can see your mind is not on Earth."

"You! Well, you're right! My mind is never on Earth."

"I wanted to thank you so much for what you've written. I've never read anything more beautiful."

"Oh! Don't worry. My pleasure."

"I've read it several times, and every time seemed exactly like the first time. It made me feel great."

"Sorry to spoil the moment, but I just remembered the pills. It's good I met you again. I forgot them. Oh, this bar! I have to run back. Would you want to join me for a beer, since I have to go back there?"

"Er … Yes, why not!" Her white cheeks turned red. She brushed her blonde hair out of her face and moved a step forward. "How did you manage to write that in such a short period of time?"

"I love writing, but I never have the time to sit down. Not everything inspires me. I could tell your eyes were a very strong stimulus. But I'll be very honest with you. Perhaps I've made you happy with my words. They're just words though. You're certainly beautiful—don't get me wrong. But my feelings weren't involved in the wording of my text. I don't know. They're just words."

"Don't worry. It's true that I kind of fell in love with your words. And having known the author made me shiver. I wish you'd written down your number so that I could have called you."

"I didn't think it was necessary. Art should be something anonymous. It shouldn't be used for business or seduction. It was a gift that you certainly deserve, unique for you. All art should be like this: images to be seen and words to be read by everyone."

"I like this point of view, and I agree."

"Please don't agree with me. I'd love for you to be more curious and contradict most of what I say. This is if you want to make every conversation we have exciting and challenging."

She nodded and smiled. They walked side by side as if they'd known each other for a very long time. There was no question asked, only points discussed. Lewis felt comfortable not having to hit on her and not desiring to take anything further than that particular conversation. He enjoyed this type of encounter. The street was always the same as everywhere, with people and faces appearing and disappearing. *A meaning of life can only be personal. It can never be summed up or defined. It's everyone's own experience, expectations, and achievements in life that can give that meaning that most never think about. How do we come to think one way or another? We've been taught most of the horrible things, and now we work. We work to live, and we work harder to have better standards.*

"This is the lounge. I was sitting by the bar," Lewis said.

"Nice place!"

"I've never been here before. But you know, what makes a place beautiful is the people you're with. Everything else is just background, just like a picture. Sorry! Let me just ask the bartender about the bag."

He spoke to the bartender, who confirmed that the bag had been taken to the office. While waiting, he ordered a whiskey for himself and a margarita for the girl. They sat down by the bar silently, as if they had to restart the conversation from the beginning.

"Thank you for the drink," she said.

"You're welcome."

"There's something about you that's blatantly saying you're a nice person."

"I don't know. I think the good hearts are always hidden." He paused for a bit. He had a sudden thought and continued. "Actually, since you mentioned my heart, I'll tell you more because I don't know you. This is maybe the last time I ever see you. Like a visit to a priest."

"You make me laugh."

"I know. The dearest to me calls me a retard."

"And you know you're not."

"This heart inside has known loneliness for a long time, although these eyes have seen and been around amazing bodies and hot women. There was a disagreement between the two, and then reason tried to get involved. This heart had been put aside and never reacted at all. One girl arrived one day, and she opened my chest and kissed my heart with blessings. It became warm and made me feel wonderful. I discovered its power and how different life was with the way it was beating. You may have experienced the same thing."

"Probably!"

"Those moments are magical. You forget about everything else. You have wings, and you fly everywhere without paying attention to where you land. All those feelings of greatness and happiness turned into rivers of tears, storms. The pain exceeded all of the joy I'd ever felt before. Dark times came. The darkened space of the universe invaded every little drop of my hopes. I ran barefoot on a harsh land where my tears were my own dreadful nightmares. I sank like a heavy rock next to worthless creatures. I was just a dead body.

"I knew that feeling of loneliness, facing dark scenes just like the sight of my horizon. I never managed to get there, and I had already lost the sight of my shore. I was in the middle of nowhere indeed. The desert of my soul had completely taken over my mind, and nothing was possible anymore. No hope, no future. I thought the water of love had drained in a dry sand, disappeared without giving any sign of life. I was doomed.

"Then I shut down everything. I stopped believing, and I confirmed, as I'd always thought, that life was indeed meaningless."

"Sorry, I wanted to say a few things in between, but I couldn't stop you."

"You don't have to say anything. I was telling you about my past, my thoughts. Well, this doesn't mean I'm much different than then. I've met beauties. I've gone out with girls but never stayed. I avoided everything that could get my heart involved—or maybe it was my heart that never wanted to get involved. I stopped breathing."

"I think everyone experiences these kinds of feelings in life. Some people even worse, depending on how strong the personality is."

"When it comes to feelings, no one can actually put their feet in the shoes of another. The pain you undergo yourself is the extreme pain. When my girl left me, I decided to give priority to my eyes and my hands. I saw beauties around, and I chased them. I spent my time with them, and then I was the one leaving. They inspired me, and I wrote when I could. I met hundreds of girls and slept with most of them. And I told myself, 'The feeling of love will never run through me again.' That's what I thought. But I'm actually in love with one girl, and I try to reject it because I want to protect her. She deserves better. I'm the worst you could be with. What's good about me? My heart! In pain or in love, it will beat until it stops. At least I don't have to let anyone feel this agony—not because of me, or not anymore."

"Don't say that. You should try with her. It might work. Does she like you?"

Lewis replied, "I saw it in her eyes the first time I met her. And what I love more about that girl is her heart, her modesty, and her honesty."

He looked at the bar and got a hold of the bartender's eyes. He took the opportunity to order a couple more shots and then carried on. "Yes, why not. We only live once. I'm alive now, not tomorrow."

"You drink quite a lot. Running away from tomorrow?"

"I don't really worry. Tomorrow will be just fine. I don't stop when I start. I have all night long to drink, to think, to wonder … to pretend that I exist."

"Life is too short indeed. We need to act quickly."

"Life is short, and I wish it was shorter because the longer a man lives, the more he suffers."

"You think and talk about so many things at the same time," the girl noted.

"Nothing is complete within me."

"You're a very nice guy; I can feel it. I just don't know why you're drowning yourself in these ideas of death and despair."

"You can't understand. Look at my face. Do I look sad? No. I'm just confessing. I needed ears to talk to. I found yours. It's not a call for help; it's just an exercise to relieve my pain."

"It's nice to hear you express yourself that way. I feel special. I think your phone's ringing."

He took his phone out and looked at the screen. Ben was calling, so he answered. "Hey! I tried to call you earlier," Lewis said. "Okay. Sure, in an hour. Sure. See you then." He turned to the girl. "One of my best friends. I wanted to see him today, and now he called."

"Of course. I can't stay too long anyway. What about her? I'm interested."

"I can't be with her. I'm scared of hurting her. I can't be with her because one day, she'll have to leave the country, and so will I. Our visas will expire. We'll both go separate ways. And if I happened to go back, nothing could reunite us. The world I come from is evil; once you enter it, nothing can bring you back. It's like a prison. I have no right to stay here. I can suffer, and that's okay, but not her. I've been with her for almost three years. No one knows about my feelings toward her—the secret of my life. We just call it friendship.

"The letters of her name are the ones mostly uttered in my head. Her face, her smile are the sunlight of my mornings. Her words are the breeze of my days. Her heart is the lullaby of my nights. Her personality is what gives me life. Her kindness is the color of my smiles. Everything about her makes me feel different. We all need to sacrifice something in life. I think she's the source of all my inspirations. That girl! I wish I was just like everyone, a free man able to choose my own faith, to live wherever I want. I wish visas didn't exist. I wish I'd been born somewhere else."

"Sorry to cut you here. Why not, though?"

"This is what you Europeans cannot understand. You know, back home in Algeria, getting a visa to come to Europe is like winning the jackpot. It happens once in a lifetime. I had my luck once. I wanted to leave my country because I couldn't stand it. I'm here now, between life and death. This is called agony. The amount of pain I have in my body is worse than that of a woman giving birth. I'm not exaggerating. Oh, sorry—I *am* exaggerating. Not the right metaphor."

She laughed.

The music coincided with his words. He felt the melancholic notes floating around in the air, words of despair and words of hope on his tongue. The usual feeling.

The girl leaned on the bar, her hand on her cheek as she stared at Lewis's lips moving in every direction. Her mind was blown away. She found within his spirit a world of love, a lost love somewhere out there in the universe of injustice. She wished she'd had someone like him, someone who could feel that way for her and only her. A man in her life would have changed things. Then she tried to forget about herself and concentrate on Lewis's adventures. Questions surfaced in her head, but for some reason, she couldn't ask them. She was happy enough just listening. She saw sincerity and good faith in his eyes. She had read and was hearing words she'd never heard before, from one man in one day. *Who's this man?* she wondered.

Lewis opened his mouth again. Like an alcoholic, the more he drank, the more he wanted it. His thoughts were easy to express, his heart beat outside, and everyone could see it. A transparent love. A beautiful landscape drawn on huge walls, impossible to miss.

"Excuse me. I'm going to the bathroom," he said.

"Sure."

He needed an escape. What was his main problem? Was it leaving the country or leaving the love of his life!? He could stay with other girls though. He could marry a European girl and get that red passport that would give him the freedom he sought, but his heart refuted those creatures. He realized that the main problem of his life was to have been born Algerian. Then again, he thought about his heart. If his heart was just like everybody else's, then he could have just stayed in his homeland with whatever culture, traditions, and taboos existing there. He could have lived there and married the first girl whom his eyes liked; he would have given her kids and fed them, raising them to become someone like him or like everybody else in the same common social environment. Because that wasn't the case, and because his mind and heart couldn't fit in, Lewis became a beggar of freedom and love, always looking for them. Like every Algerian, he could find them only abroad. He managed to find his freedom. He found his love at the end but couldn't have it. The boundaries were closed by his fear of going back to Algeria.

He washed his face without looking in the mirror. He wiped his hands and dried himself before he went back to the bar. His phone rang again, and he remembered Ben. *Oh, shit! I'm sure this is Ben. I said one hour. Time goes by so fast.*

He answered, "Yes, sorry, I'm running late. Are you there? Okay, okay, yeah. Sorry. See you in a bit."

"Has he been waiting all this time?" she asked.

"This is what he said, but I'm sure he wasn't. Otherwise, he would have called me the moment he got there. He's always late himself. Well, listen, I need to get going. I'm very glad I've met you and spoken to you. I feel fine. Maybe I'll pop in one day and say hi."

"Yes, sure! And thank *you*. It was great meeting you."

"Take care." He moved closer and opened his arms. "A free hug?" He smiled and gave her a tight hug. "Life is all around you. Don't miss out," he added. He let go of her, smiled again, and then disappeared in the crowd.

Ben was waiting for him in another bar. They hadn't seen a lot of each other recently. Lewis took the underground and got there as quickly as he could.

Once inside the bar, he saw Ben playing on his phone, two beers on the table. He'd already finished one, if not more. The place was full of people, and many were squeezed together at the counter trying to get a drink. Lewis walked close to Ben and gave him a tap on the head.

"Hey! Your head is always down! Look at the world around you."

"Please! Whom am I going to look at?"

"No wonder you're still single."

Ben got up and gave Lewis a hug.

"I missed you, brother," he said.

"I missed you too, you little shit."

"What's new?" Ben said.

"Same old shit."

"Anyway, what do you want to drink?"

"Finish that beer quickly, and let's go somewhere else. I need to talk to you."

"Sure."

Ben grabbed his beer, looked at it, and then looked at Lewis. He smiled and then poured it all down his throat. He wiped his face with his arm and said, "Let's hear what you have to say. You're a stranger these days."

"You've got to be kidding me."

"That's how I feel."

"Let's walk to Oxford Street."

"Long way."

"I know where we are."

It was a cold night in London, and everyone wore coats, scarves, and gloves except for the girls—English girls. It felt like a parade outside. Different people dressed up differently, and people had their own styles and their own ways of life. He could see freedom written on their foreheads. No one needed to pretend to be something else, and no one else was bothered if others pretended to be someone else. Lights, always lights. It never felt like nighttime until they got into a club. People and cars everywhere. The streets were very full. The world looked happy, at least from the outside. Lewis looked happy, and so was Ben.

"I don't need to start," Ben said. "You always talk to me. Because you said you had to talk to me, which means there's something important to bring up. Your silence makes it obvious."

"Since when do you reason that way?"

"Since I've noticed a change in your behavior. Get straight to the point."

"I love her."

"I knew it," Ben replied without any change in his facial expression or the tone of his voice.

"Is it that obvious?"

"You're no longer the same. I always have fun with you when I go out, but lately you've seemed to stop yourself from going to the edge. Something is calling you all the time. Something is reminding you and holding you back, not allowing you to cross the bridge on which you used to run."

"I don't know. She's taken me progressively, like ants eating a dead body."

"You know it's a forbidden love."

Lewis nodded. "I know."

"Don't let it destroy the dream you're after."

"Fuck! What dream?"

"You know exactly what I'm talking about," Ben said. "Do you want to end up here like me? I'm dead. I have no future. My visa has expired, I can't find a woman to marry, I can't travel, I can't go see my family, and I can't get a job I want. You want to join me behind the sink? If your visa expires, you're done. Done! You understand? If I were you with all those girls you meet, I wouldn't have hesitated a second. I would have married any one of them to settle down first. Only then can you really grasp a taste of freedom. Don't be silly. Love has no room in our lives at the moment."

"We're going to Vienna together next weekend. She's booked everything."

"It's a mistake. Don't go. Something bad will happen, and you'll be stuck forever. You'll follow your heart, and you'll be fucked. Or you will follow your reason and will still be fucked. Close the doors to your heart and throw the keys into the deepest oceans."

"No more."

"Exactly. I have no more to say. You understand perfectly."

"I know."

"You'll end up hurting her, and hurting yourself, in every way."

Lewis kept quiet, walking in the desert of perplexity. Nothing more could be said. Nothing more could be done. But he'd already decided to go away with her. If death were to come, then at least he'd have spent the last moments with the person who deserved more than his presence. Like a cancer, his date was almost due, so he decided to enjoy it the way his heart requested.

"Let's go to M2 Club," Ben said.

"Do you have something to smoke?"

"What a question!"

"Ha-ha, great."

There could be two different lives behind a smiling face, a happy one or a sad one, Lewis thought.

Both Lewis and Ben knew how the course of the night would be. A series of the same scenes that always happened was about to unfold. Go to a bar, flirt with girls, smoke some joints, and then end up in the toilet sniffing some shit. First, shake hands with the security guys. Ben did the same. Lewis couldn't be the only one to shake hands there; it wouldn't make sense to those people without Ben. There always had to be first Lewis and then Ben, unless one of them was already waiting for the other inside. They went in to hear the same music and see the same people with different faces, and of course one or two new waitresses. The full bar wasn't a problem. Lewis waved to someone, someone waved back, and already two drinks were in his hands. Ben refreshed the area with his big smile, but people were ignoring him, so he ignored them too.

A sudden tap on Lewis's back made him turn around. "No fucking way!" he exclaimed. "This is a joke."

"It might appear so, but it's real."

The music was loud, and they hardly heard each other.

Lewis introduced Ben to his old friend Anthony, and they chatted for a bit. Anthony warmly invited them to join him and some friends at his table, and Lewis accepted."

"Ben, let's go," Lewis said.

"I'm following."

On their way, in the middle of the crowd, Ben pulled Lewis by his shirt to slow him down. He got closer to Lewis's ear and said, "Who's this guy?"

"I'll tell you later."

"Tell me now."

"God, he's an old colleague, that's all. He used to love this girl who always ignored him but loved another one."

"Not surprised."

"Just shut up and follow me."

Anthony walked in the front. He was a tall man, wide and heavy, and he made the way through the crowd very easy for the two behind. The table seemed to be at the other end of the club, where the VIP area was. It was not very surprising because Anthony's mother was a top model, quite wealthy, and aristocratic. There were two security guys blocking the entrance to the VIP area. They moved to the side as soon as Anthony got closer.

"They're with me," he said.

"Hey, Lewis! What's up?" one of Anthony's guards said.

"Good, man! Good to see you too, always."

"Never lost the fame," Anthony added.

Lewis shrugged and stepped forward. Ben shook both their hands and then quickly followed inside. The lights in the VIP area were darker. Champagne and vodka bottles weren't just decorations on the table. Girls danced topless in their miniskirts. Hot girls were everywhere, too busy with party animals.

"Look at that corner over there," Anthony said.

"No fucking way! Ben!" Lewis poked him.

"Can I have a shot, please?" Ben replied.

Some famous football players were throwing a party, pouring champagne in some girls' mouths and all over their faces, the champagne dripping onto their boobs. They looked pretty sexy.

"Do you want a line?" Anthony said.

"Yes!" Ben startled. "In these kinds of situations? Yes, fuck!"

"Not yet," Lewis said. "I haven't drunk that much yet. But you can have one with Ben. He loves it."

They both left for the bathroom. Lewis sat down, poured some vodka lime and lemonade, and looked around but ignored everything, even the footballers. Temptation and desires streamed around. It could almost be seen drifting between legs and arms, rising in the air, and taking reason to dark cells. Only animals were left down there—hungry bodies, ready to erect. He had another shot, then a second one. Ben and Anthony were back.

"I'll have a line as well."

"Sure, take this."

They discreetly grabbed each other's hands and exchanged the small plastic bag. There was more than two grams; he could feel it by the space it took up in his hand. It was so early, and almost everyone was drunk. The bathroom was full, with people queuing inside for the same reason. He had two lines.

Ben was dancing, and he let his body express his Algerian frustration, a poor man next to the richest he could ever meet. This could have been called freedom, it could have been called savagery, or it could have been called anything. Only he knew what it really meant, legs and hands in the air, the way one had never seen anywhere else. Everyone looked at him, but he seemed to be dancing by himself in an empty room. His nose was red because he kept scratching it. His eyes were hanging and his face was pale, a zombie coming to life.

Lewis said, "Hey, Anthony! Shall we go for a cigarette?"

"Sure."

They went upstairs to the smoking area and lit their cigarettes.

"Long time no see," Lewis said.

"I know. We moved to New York. I've just come back to see some old friends."

"What happened to Tania?"

"She broke my heart and left. She managed to find a nice man; he works in fashion. She's fine now, quite happy. And I am happy for her. I have moved on."

"My friend, there are no other options. The world is full of nice women. You will find one someday just like you, smart and classy."

"Thanks. Are you still the same playboy?"

"I'm not a playboy. I'm a man who's looking for a treasure. The treasure is inside a room that's locked. Do you know how many rooms are there? Plenty, so I have to open them one by one until I find it."

"And you still haven't found it?" Anthony asked.

"I think I have. I just need to know whether the treasure itself is my property."

"What are you doing here, then?"

"My friend wanted a drink, so I came with him. Have you seen any girls around me tonight?"

"Not yet."

"It's not going to happen. I'm leaving soon anyway."

"Let's go back downstairs."

"We need some shots."

Lewis wanted to love, and the love he felt was hard to explain. *Sometimes you love, and you don't know why you love. It's the same for a newborn baby. Parents love their child no matter what it looks like, no matter what it will grow up to be, no matter what it does.*

That miracle of love hadn't happened to Tania and Anthony. She'd had to give up and couldn't take it anymore. She'd gone mad and disappeared without a word. Anthony had lived moments in anguish and despised himself, believing that his love story had been spoiled by his wealth.

Ben was sitting on the sofa, and two girls kissed him at the same time. It looked like an erotic mist. Lewis didn't want to call him. He'd had two shots and a third one for Ben's amusement. The drug started taking effect, and the alcohol felt like water. He could carry on drinking all night. He clenched his fists, an d his mouth felt numb. *Ben's having fun, anyway.* It was already too late. He left the place without letting anybody know. He headed to Aylin's place. He'd promised he'd go see her that night. He obviously hadn't meant to go that late, and she must have expected him at a more decent hour.

He tried to ignore the idea. He stopped a cab and got into it. *I'm sorry, Ben.*

The door was closed. She came to open it as soon as he'd knocked, although she'd been sleeping. Her hair was all messed up, her skin looked soft, and her eyes were only half open. She wore his favorite light black dress and a jumper with long sleeves. She looked so innocent and beautiful.

"Sorry, I was with Ben. I had to run away from him."

"It's okay. Come in."

"Were you sleeping?"

"Lewis, it's almost 3:00 a.m. I didn't think you'd be coming."

"I know—stupid question. Let's go eat."

"No! I'm sleepy."

"Come on! It's okay, you're free tomorrow. You'll have all day to sleep."

He grabbed her hand and pulled her to the kitchen. He felt good. It was good to be around her. He made some eggs, toasted some bread, and told her the truth about the course of his night. Shortly after, she told him that she had to go to bed. That moment was longer than any he'd spent out somewhere else. He kissed her on the forehead and wished her a good night. He went to the balcony and had a few cigarettes. The sun was rising, and he felt the breeze of the morning shaking his bones. He remained there, thinking.

His phone rang. *Ben.*

"Hey, man! What the fuck?"

"Sorry. I saw you having a good time. I was tired and didn't want to ruin your night. Have you just come out?"

"Fuck you, man. You've never done this to me before. I was looking around for you. I thought maybe someone was blowing your cock somewhere. I waited outside until everyone left the club, and you never came out."

"Sorry, brother. Anyway, you sound so fucked. Go home. The tube must be open."

"So you're with Aylin!? That girl will fuck you up. Go get married, you fucking asshole. You have five months until your visa expires. What the fuck are you going to do?"

"Ben!" Lewis replied, raising his voice. "Forget it. We'll speak tomorrow."

"Fuck off," Ben replied, and he hung up.

Lewis sighed. He threw away the rest of his cigarette and went to Aylin's room. He watched her sleep for a moment. He smiled and then went to the second bedroom. He fell asleep as soon as his head touched the pillow.

Maybe he didn't have enough choices in his life. Maybe he didn't have the best fate, the best destiny. Maybe he didn't know where he was going or where he'd end up in five months time. However, he knew exactly what he wanted. He couldn't promise anything. He couldn't open his mouth and express his thoughts and feelings. What he wanted was precious and at the same time too complicated. What he wanted was almost his, but he didn't dare get hold of it. It was a sort of protection that caused more pain than anything. The pain was worth it if it meant keeping his friend next to him.

Chapter 9

"If we are the virus of this world, then love is ours. Not the
love for others—it's the love for ourselves, selfishness."

The night had taken him nowhere. Everything was blank when he woke
up the next day. His head spun, and his hands shook. He'd had too many
drinks, consumed too many drugs. He felt tired and remained in bed. The
best moment in life was rest. He stretched his legs and arms for a moment
but finally decided to get up. Aylin was still sleeping. He didn't want to
wake her up. He ate something and then went back to sleep. He changed
his mind. Nothing to wake up for. Her place was the only place where he
could rest. When he woke up again, it was dark. Dark times, dark life. He
saw a piece of paper on the table.

> I didn't want to wake you up. I'll be out for dinner with some
> friends. There's some food in the fridge; you just need to warm it
> up. You can stay if you want to. I'll speak to you later.

He grabbed a pen and wrote underneath her message, "Thanks."
He ate some food, trying not to think of anything, but Ben's words
couldn't be ignored. There was a bit of wisdom in his words. *He's probably*
right. I love this girl, she's amazing, and we'd be so good together. But I should
face the truth and realize that everything is a lie. My visa expires very soon.
I'll have to go back to my country, where I obviously cannot survive. Besides,
she'll have to go back as well. She's a student, and her visa expires just after
mine. None of us can help the other stay. I don't think I can go live in her
country, although sometimes I want to keep it as an option. Her country is
similar to mine, a third-world country. She'd never come with me to my land.

I wouldn't allow her to come. There's a smell of misery and death on my land. What can I do?

I wish I could have a life—the one I could choose myself. I'm surrounded by obstacles. I'm surrounded by shrinking walls restricting my view. My life seems to be coming to an end very soon. Not even five months left. Feels like a boat running to a waterfall, and I can already see it. Should I call for help? Who's going to listen? What kind of help am I going to look for? Do I have other choices? I need to get married. It's the only thing I can do to stay here and maybe save our relationship. Would she wait for me, though? Shall I just live with it and never unveil the secret of my heart to her? She shouldn't know, then. I have to get married. I have to find someone to help me stay. A fake marriage! But who? All those girls I've been with loved me. I've slept with each of them. They'd never say yes. If they did want to marry me, it would be to make me stay with them. I wouldn't want any of them to stay with me because I want to live with someone else. Maybe I'll try those girls I didn't take to bed because I didn't want to, because they were not my style, not my taste. There aren't many of them, though. I need a friend. Who is my friend? I need a good heart. Who has one?

He'd made up his mind. He decided to give it a try. It was so easy and yet too hard. He simply needed to find someone who'd marry him for the papers, nothing more—a contract just to stay in the country. He was even willing to pay money for it, as most other immigrants did. He thought the sooner, the better, but he'd never tell Aylin. He was scared of losing her. He'd have to explain that his heart was with her.

He opened her laptop and checked his Facebook. He selected some girls he could potentially ask. It was obviously the hardest thing he'd have to do. What to say and how to say it? His mind was empty, and he couldn't write anything.

His phone rang; it was Mary.

"Hi, Mary! How are you?"

"Hi, Lewis! Long time no speak! I'm good. How are you?"

"Not bad. Struggling as always. What's new?"

"I've found a job. I work in a shipping company, and I love it. Busy though. I have no life. You?"

"Oh, you know, the usual shit. I'm not working these days. I feel lazy."

"Tell me about it. Just called to say hi. Let's catch up very soon."

"Sure! I'll let you know when I'm free."

"Great. Speak soon. Ciao."

"Ciao."

He thought about mentioning his situation to Mary. The words wouldn't come out of his mouth. It wasn't that easy. It couldn't be that simple. *Hey! How are you? Would you marry me because I want to stay in this country?* It was too absurd.

He put on his clothes and left the place, heading nowhere. He wandered around until midnight. His blood was calling for the taste of alcohol, but he tried hard to ignore it. He decided to go to his cold home, where he was all alone in his empty space and had to face the truth. He poured a glass of whiskey and sat down on a chair next to the window. *The same things every day, and they're decaying.* He opened his laptop and chose a contact from his Facebook contact list. He gave it a long thought and came up with a conclusion. *I've nothing to lose. Let's say I've already lost everything.* He started writing.

Liking is a natural phenomenon. It happens when we least expect it—a profound reaction to a stimulus that either pokes you all of a sudden or grows inside of you over time. But why do we like, and whom do we like? Liking nowadays has changed from what it was before. Malice has taken over, ruling over our lives. It used to be naive, sincere, and honest. It was easy, spontaneous, and unconditional. Today, all these words are vanishing, dying out. Other words come to fruition that are the disease of humankind: interest, materialism, expectations, deception, artifice. This is how people tend to like for one reason or another nowadays, but never for the love of our personalities or thoughts. We are condemned to live with these people today. Does it mean that we have to be just like them? What about those people who need help from us? What about me, in need of help from other people who wouldn't have to sacrifice but a word? We all need help at some point. But the world has different opposing sides: north, south, east, and west. Exactly how life's fairness is split up. Exactly the way things are made, to be different.

I'm Algerian, after all. Who cares about my faith? Who cares about what I know or can achieve? Nobody. I can tell you the thought is digging inside my heart. I'm no longer able to recognize myself. I'm too different as well.

True liking or love is when we do everything to make people around us happy without expecting anything back. Even friends are fake now. I've known them; I've given them the chance to stand by my side, the chance to make them feel free and comfortable. At least, I thought they were friends, but I guess I misunderstood the real meaning of friendship. They all let me down when I tried to call their names. I needed a shoulder to cry on; they all stepped back. No more friends. What's left is company. We're here to laugh, to joke, to drink. Tomorrow doesn't belong to anyone, and nobody thinks about it. I might see you the next day. I might be there on that date. Those feelings you get, those emotions that take you to a lost landscape. Nothing is to be said. Nothing is to be heard. The world has changed, and so has the climate, as well as the path we're meant to follow.

Until now, you might say, "What is he talking about?" But it's too hard to say it because maybe I shouldn't. I'm left without any choice. If you could understand the torment of my words, then maybe you'd be brave enough to talk to me. But never expect anything from anyone. This is my philosophy. I need to ask you a favor. I've tried everyone I know. Nobody cared.

Sorry for the long message. I hope you're good.

He copied and sent it to many different girls. He didn't mind at all. *I have no other choice, and I have nothing to lose. I'd rather never see these faces again than lose Aylin.*

He closed his laptop, drank his whiskey, and started praying like he'd never had to something out there, no matter what it was.

His phone was turned off. He waited for hours while drinking and smoking. He fell asleep on the chair and kept waking up and checking whether there was any answer. He messaged Aylin to let her know he was fine and had things to do at home. He spent all his time sleeping and checking his phone. Two days, three days, but no answer from anyone. He'd been let down by everyone.

The moment he didn't expect it anymore, a message appeared in his inbox. *Anna!*

Lewis,

"True liking or love is when we do everything to make people around us happy without expecting anything back." That sentence hit me like a stone in the heart. I just reread your message, and I'm shivering. Your point of view is so true. Sad, but true. I wish I could tell you that your life is wonderful, that love will win over everything, and that it's always worth fighting for, but I know you won't believe me. A part of me totally agrees with you. I know it's true; this is the reality of life, of people, of our society. But another part tells me that the power of life can't be forgotten. We're lucky to be alive, to be part of this world. We have the opportunity to do something in our lives, to build, to experiment; these things will feed our personality. We're lucky to have a certain knowledge, a certain consciousness of what's around and inside us. I don't know whether I'll be able to explain myself, but what I mean is that we're the creators of our lives. To some extent, we can choose, and we can decide to be, to become, to behave the way we want to. This is freedom.

Those things are extremely important to me. They give me the power to fight for myself, to stand up, and to go on again and again. I'm like you (to be honest, I try to be), and I don't expect anything from anyone … except from me.

I'm waiting for you. Please tell me how I can help you, how I can be there for you. I'll do everything I can to help you. Really!

Kiss.

Lewis sighed after reading the message. He should have said it right away. Yes, to avoid these discussions. *Freedom! Choosing! You don't know what it's like to be born in a country like Algeria!* he thought.

He crafted his reply.

Hey! Thanks. First, I didn't expect an answer from you at all. I've read my message again and realized how long it was and how vague and deep it might appear. Your answer sounds sincere, and I appreciate it a lot. So, thank you once again in the middle of my speech.

You mentioned a few things that I'd like to comment on, but I won't have enough space for that. You know, some African tribes still worship the snake, even nowadays, because they believe that the snake has known Earth with its entire body, from head to toe. I read that in a book called Zorba the Greek by Nikos Kazantzakis. It's a very amazing interpretation of life itself. But who has experienced it all that way? I have personalized life, and I know that life can never be my friend until I submit. I choose not to because I'm aware that freedom is the real governor of life itself, so I feed myself from its energy. I try to get hold of it, but I never managed to acquire the whole body. Now, I know the taste, but the whole meal is forbidden. For some people, the extent of freedom has limits. Those people live with a different interpretation of freedom in order to keep going: they smile, they sing, they dance. Beyond those instinctive, natural desires and ambitions, there's an empty space—nothing but space. When we're conscious of those spaces, we end up sad no matter how much we try not to be.

I'm sorry for being a bit vague with my words. I can't express myself explicitly; this is what I learned from life. I'm playing all my cards. Otherwise, I'll always be the loser.

It's been years since I came to this country. I came for two reasons: to finish my studies and to work. I'd say my graduation was the best achievement of my life. I won't tell you about my broken heart from different perspectives. Everyone in life goes through these stages and learns from them. Yes, I've been in love, the world of magical emotions, the tricky feeling. The stronger it is, the worse the consequences are. I ended up in torments. It wasn't a nightmare. If that was the punishment of humankind, then I'd do it a hundred times over. Gibran Khalil Gibran said, "Joy and Sorrow are inseparable. Together they come, and when one sits alone with you at your board, remember that the other is asleep upon your bed." I'm seeing a girl now, and she's the most amazing person I've ever met. I have the potential for getting a great job and growing higher, but all of this seems to end soon. I cannot be more honest.

My visa will expire in four months, and I'll have to go back and leave behind this world of freedom. Go back to the hell where evil has settled. I've checked all possibilities to stay in the country, but because the immigration law has changed, I'm left with only one option: to marry someone in order to stay. I could pretend to love someone and marry her. I could play a whole game and convince a girl to marry me. But my heart does not allow me to do so. I can't be a source of destruction, and no soul should have to bear the pain of my ego or joy. So I thought my friends would be able to help me. I asked. I said I was looking for a soul like mine who can understand, but I saw none. Then you came to my mind. I thought, *I have an instinctive feeling that she might help me.*

These are my words to you. Now that you know, please don't feel like you're in a bad position where you'd regret anything. You don't have to do anything. I'm already flattered by your response, so thank you again. By marriage, I mean help me to get my documents. I know it sounds crazy, but it's doable. I know people who've done it before.

Take care of yourself.

Sincerely,
Lewis

Very wrong, he thought as he pressed on the send button. Wrong as everything was meant to be. Images of the past crossed his mind. He hadn't chosen to be born where he'd been born. He hadn't chosen to come to the UK. He'd been forced to run away from his country. He couldn't choose the woman of his life. He couldn't travel as much as he wished. He couldn't tell the truth about himself to most people. He couldn't be a dreamer. He couldn't wish for anything at all. Reality was too harsh for him. But it was also fine because at the same time, he couldn't really complain. He couldn't change his present. He had to face those facts, those emotions. He had to be there anyway—that day, on that chair, in his house. He'd lost all his hope and didn't give a damn about life anymore. He called for death to come. *Take me. What are you waiting for?* Every day was the same. Every day was a hill to mount. Every day was a burden. He was a victim of God's fate.

He remained on his chair, drinking again. Sometimes he tried to imagine a tomorrow, his future, but it was blank and black. Nothing came to his mind. There was nothing there but death. Death was an escape not from the rules of truth but from what man himself had invented. Four days already he'd spent at home. He ate less but drank more. He slept less but raved more between love and reason, between future and past. Nobody answered. The girl didn't reply. He'd fired all his bullets. There was nothing else left. He left because he wanted a drink outside. He needed that fresh air. He needed to feel free. He needed to do the simple things at least. Choosing a bar. Choosing someone's company. Choosing a drink and a seat.

He sat down in one corner and drank shots and beer. He felt better. He saw some people he knew; he heard some music he liked. What he did was leave that place—always the same things, always. He walked, and he didn't stop walking. He headed to Aylin's. It took him hours before he got there. She was sleeping because she'd had a long day. He got onto the bed and went to sleep as well. He felt exhausted.

He spent the rest of the week at her place. Nothing could be more peaceful.

"We're leaving tomorrow? I'm going home to get my stuff, and I'll be back," Lewis said.

"Okay. I'm lazy."

"Tell me something new."

"Shut up and let me sleep."

"All right, see you later."

Daylight outside—that didn't happen very often. He felt weird walking in bright light, in sunlight, seeing bright faces and puppies and parents with strollers. He could see the things he normally didn't have a chance to see at night. The warmth of the sun affected his feelings. He'd visited a wonderful world to which he'd never belonged. The holiday had started already.

He needed a small bag: underwear, shirts, two or three pairs of jeans, and jumpers just in case. Vienna could be cold. He never needed a lot of time to get ready. He had passport in hand, and the booking was on Aylin. *Oh, flip-flops and perfume. Now, I'm ready to go.*

Ben was working and couldn't see him. He thought about calling him after work.

I never thought I'd go to Vienna one day. A beautiful city that contributed to various forms of art in the world, particularly music. As a very big fan of Mozart and Sigmund Freud, the founder of the famous psychoanalysis, I think it's worth walking on the land these great pioneers and many others have lived on. The stroll will be overwhelming because of the beauty of the baroque architecture tingling with the incredible charm of Aylin. It will be a walk in heaven.

He was already picturing his holiday. He smiled for a little while but then stopped. He wished things between Aylin and him had been just a story of friendship. He wished he could be there for her anytime and anywhere. He wished this and that. He wanted this and that, just to keep her by his side. But the truth was he truly loved her.

He knocked on the door, and she opened.

"Hey! It took you too long!" she said.

"You slept too much!"

"I needed it."

"Why Vienna?" Lewis asked.

"We're actually going somewhere else. I changed my mind and booked tickets to Sardinia."

"What? Aylin, you should have told me. I would have brought summer stuff."

"You could just buy two extra shorts and T-shirts. They're very cheap there."

"It's not just about that. You know what we call mental readiness? I need some psychological preparation. I need to know what kind of weather I'll be facing, what kind of people I'll be talking to. I need to know for the sake of knowing."

"I thought you were one of those guys who like to go with the flow. Where's your spontaneity?"

"I don't know, lack of patience. Besides, I'm already with the flow. You said we go, and I said yes. Where to go makes a difference. I don't want to spend money on things I already have. Well, I won't spoil the moment. Let's make something to eat."

"Good boy! You cook, and I'll paint."

"That's fine, as long as you're washing the dishes!"

"As always, asshole."

They laughed together. What a very special moment. Who would think a simple scene like that could make someone dream? Both seemed happily united, but both knew things between them were complicated. Their relationship was complicated.

Everything was available in the kitchen; Lewis started enjoying his improved cooking skills. Aylin sat down on the floor in the living room. She put on some exotic music and began mixing colors on a white board. A peaceful moment was recording in Lewis's memory. He rarely cooked for himself; he hated wasting time in the kitchen or even eating at a table. It was a different story, cooking for her. The time flew by quickly, and the food was soon ready. He set the table and called Aylin to eat. He lit two candles, put on some Mark Knopfler, and opened a French red wine. Romance was the biggest part of his life. The fineness of the atmosphere made him forget about the outside world. The taste of the food, the smell of the wine, the waving shadows of their bodies on the walls—every detail made the moment exceptional. How did he feel? He felt good, comfortable. They talked about memories, his conquests, and her drama. It couldn't have been better. He teased her, she got upset, he laughed, and she laughed. She annoyed him, he didn't mind, and they laughed again and again while facing each other.

"To tomorrow!" Lewis raised his glass.

"To life, forever," she replied.

A cold wind struck Lewis's heart. With her bow, she'd pulled the arrow very hard, pointed at the target, and let it go. She'd violently hit the beat of his compassion. He'd stopped breathing but tried to be discreet. He smiled and took a long sip to stop the fire in his body. Smoke could have come out of his nose and ears. The words she'd used, *life* and *forever*, together in one breath.

What is forever? We will die. One of us will die first. Nothing is forever if one of us dies. It can't be. It's a lie. What if there's a life after death? How can you look behind? What would you see? A broken heart you promised to be with forever, devastated because you realize it couldn't be forever. And life! What is life? Is it just this moment? It could be, but then again, it can't last forever. I'll leave. I can't stay with you, Aylin. I can't hurt you. Life is harsh on us. I don't want to be part of the life-inspiring injustice, and I don't want to be that life that leaves you alone, that life that can't be without you.

"What are you thinking about?" Aylin asked.

"What a question to ask. I don't know; my brain never stops working. I was thinking about so many things at the same time. Picturing everything like a satellite watching Earth. I think about today and about tomorrow's trip. Besides, you know, no one would ever tell you what he's truly thinking about when you surprisingly ask a question like that."

"Ha-ha, don't be an asshole."

"I'm serious. We struggle hard to express our thoughts, especially in some specific circumstance. So when we get asked that question, we get scared and panic. You suspect the person to understand something or feel concerned in your thoughts, and then the fear blocks you even more from expressing the thought. Therefore whatever we respond is a lie. Don't ask the question and let the truth come to you. You'll appreciate it more."

"The same way you just lied!"

"Don't use everything I say against me. I might have lied. Lies aren't always bad."

"A lie is a lie."

"I know. But you should know that sometimes you have to lie to prevent something from happening. You have to lie to protect the truth. It could also be called hiding the truth instead of lying."

"You can hide as long as you're not asked to reveal the truth. The moment you're asked and say the opposite of a thought or a fact, it becomes a lie."

"You could save a life by lying—that's all I know. Now, whether saying the truth is better than saving a life, it's up to you to judge. Moreover, every human being lies. It's part of our nature. You've lied several times. It doesn't make you a liar. Have you ever heard of Koko the Gorilla?"

"No, I haven't."

"Koko the Gorilla learned sign language. Once, when the trainer came to visit, she found the sink was torn out of the wall. She signed to him, 'Who's torn the sink out of the wall?' Koko responded, 'The kitten has.'"

"You and your stupid jokes."

"It's not a joke! We naturally lie."

They laughed.

They finished eating and sipped the last drops of wine. Lewis went to the balcony and lit his favorite cigarette: the one after a meal. He couldn't speak to Ben; he was still working. Ben's words had never left his mind. *Regret? Regret what? Damn, I don't know anymore.*

Going back home where he had come from was impossible. Knowing where he came from, and remembering his past, wasn't something that could help him remain with Aylin. *Better to lie.* The truth about his plans to get married could only hurt. He thought of all those years he had been with her as a friend, all those moments of joy and prosperity that blossomed in his heart because of her. And he thought of all those moments he was pushing her away by flirting with women while with her and telling her about his sexual adventures. It was despair, just to hide his feelings. And all of that was a lie. He knew that engaging in a relationship with her would drive both of them into an unavoidable torture. What to do? He simply let it be and decided to remain her friend for those last moments. Life wasn't worth anything, and everything was a joke, but that smile of hers was real. Her smile could be the cure of his life. *But ...*

He felt the need for a beer but ignored it. He checked on Aylin who was getting her luggage ready. A small suitcase wasn't enough. She liked to take care of herself. She liked to look beautiful but still kept her modesty, with both feet on the ground. She'd bought a few things online: bikini, towels, and sun cream. Her face was always full of joy. Her charm was very expressive, a philosopher in this modern era.

And every time Lewis looked at her face, he got a deeper interpretation, a face full of life and mystery, a face that looked like the structure of the universe. There was so much someone would want to know about, so much to explore, and so much love to be found. The little gaze of hers was absorbing his soul. She was sucking all of his vitality out of him, and he didn't mind giving it to her. He felt like leaving his body and merging with hers to form one entity. He couldn't. Everything was a lie.

Lewis's phone rang.

"I'll be back," he said.

"Okay, but I'll sleep soon though. Our flight is early in the morning."

"Okay." He smiled.

He answered the phone. It was an Algerian friend.

"Hey, Leila. What's up?"

"Man, I'm drowning in problems. I swear."

"We all are, Leila! You can tell me more about it when I come back from my holiday. I want to go with a fresh mind. Anything very urgent, or just the usual shit?"

"Usual shit."

"Okay, then, we'll discuss it later." He hung up and sighed.

Trouble, trouble, trouble. Who on Earth doesn't have a problem? Whomever you try to confess to has worse than you can ever imagine. Who will listen? Everyone is on the same boat. People find complaining so easy. They open their mouths to share, as if the solutions lie in someone else's hands. Surely they know what they'll hear. Is it in order to hear the same stories back? I don't know. To feel more comfortable because someone else has a harder life and bigger problems? Everyone has his own problems. I was in love once; she left me. The one I crave for is right next to me, and I can't be with her. My visa will expire soon; I have to go back to hell. I don't have a job; I quit. I spent the rest of my money drinking alcohol and taking drugs. This is my shit, and the solutions should be within me or around me. I am the only one who can help myself. Damn, this is hard.

On the other hand, are we not responsible for most of the choices we're making? I could stop drinking and taking drugs. I could reveal my feelings to Aylin. I could go back to Algeria and take her with me, or I could go to her hometown. I'd live wherever I'd have the chance to, as long as I have her love locked in my heart. But I'm selfish like everyone else. I want everything. We all know this. What's everybody's role in this world? Who knows? Maybe we're the most dangerous virus for this planet, this universe. Eating from it, multiplying and changing its nature. Reason? What reason? To kill each other for food and luxury. What a selfish person a human being can be! Now we're here, pretending we're happy when things go right and moaning all the time for a better meal, a better house, and a perfect woman. None of this shit should exist. Because we exist, nothing else is to be expected. We're the enemies of nature.

Love! If we're a virus to nature, then love is a virus to us. Not the love for others—it's the love for ourselves, selfishness. We like to feel different inside by a stimulus that could be anything. Nothing will last, not even that first feeling. It dies. And another one comes to life for a different thing, a different person. Love drives men crazy. We like ourselves too much to be able to choose who could be with us. Otherwise, everything's equal, everyone's human, everyone fucks, and everyone eats and laughs. We look for much to satisfy our own ego. What have we done to ourselves? If there was a God, then that God doesn't have any power. If he was that powerful, then he could have put an end to this race and change it into another race without a brain, without greed, without desires. He could have suppressed the ego, the arrogance and intelligence, and that race could live like other animals.

I'd prefer to say that God doesn't exist because if he does, then he's not fair—he's harsh and not treating us equally. If he existed, then it is fair to say that destiny exists too, and if he was the one to decide where we're born, then he obviously gives to some the chance to live happy lives, and he condemns others to lead miserable lives. To be born in the United Kingdom and in Iraq is what I call heaven and hell, respectively. Is he really fair? Is this to test people, to see how faithful they are to him? Then the test itself is wrong; it can't be right. We're not given the same obstacles; we're not given the same path. To be born with a disability is a crime. What kind of faith can God expect from a disabled person, an orphan, a holocaust survivor, or a slave? God, if he existed, would never do that. A creator should love his world and give it the best he can. Why would he make his own creation suffer from injustice? A cruel punishment. Can he expect from someone to live his whole life in pain and sorrow and yet still pray to him and thank him every day for the promise of a beautiful paradise? Why would he? Hell is what he's living in. Who's the God who would forbid you something in life in order to allow it in heaven? If something is bad, then it's bad everywhere, even in heaven!

God, where are you? Can't you cure this disease? What's your power? Death? Some people think they're alive. They're dead to me. The darkness on their faces has made them an absolute failure. They never smile, and they see horrible scenes of crimes and war. They see parents, sons, and families tortured and killed in front of their eyes. Did they choose their faith? How can they find faith in those horrors?

Faith is no longer to be found within God. Faith can only be found in a person, in the love of your life. It could be your family, a job, or a hobby. Faith is the goal that helps you get up in the morning. It gives you happiness and conjures a constant smile on your face. You're in the world, and you know why. Everything else—superstition, religion, and any other beliefs—is just your own creation for your own annihilation.

He realized how late he'd stayed outside when he pulled the last cigarette from his pack. He checked the time: only one hour left before the taxi was to arrive. He was meant to rest and be fresh to enjoy the whole trip, but his mind wasn't able to find peace. There were voices that didn't stop calling him. There were questions that raised issues he didn't want to debate. He couldn't help it. He smoked his last cigarette, sent a long message to Ben, checked his bag, and went to take a shower. He woke Aylin up; the taxi had arrived. He fell asleep. He slept all the way to the airport and then again on the plane.

Chapter 10

"A heart that feels has no brain to think."

"Wake up, you little shit. We're here," Aylin said.

"Really? Nice. It's like a dream. I fell asleep in the UK and woke up in Sardinia."

The mild wind from the Mediterranean Sea washed his face and woke him up from his sleep. It brought him back to an old memory—home. He walked next to Aylin as if they were on clouds. He contemplated every path they took. The sun was right in the middle, and the air was fresh and pure. It looked very summery. The streets were full; many people seemed to be visiting the area, free people from everywhere. Most of them were white. Getting a tan was the reason most people were there.

They were already at the hotel. The taxi had been quick and cheap. The receptionist was very hot and spoke English. He gave her a little wink and then realized Aylin was looking at him. He smiled.

"You started already!" she said.

"What? I haven't done anything."

"I know you very well."

"Isn't this a holiday? We're here to have fun."

He smiled, but Aylin's discontent was easy to distinguish. He had to do that. He had to push her away. Better that way than being with her and not being able to promise her anything. She deserved better. Aylin was not to be hurt. He started acting like a retard, Aylin laughed, and they walked to the lift. On the third floor, their room with a balcony faced the seaside. Lewis opened the window and took a deep breath. There was only one double bed, so they had to share. *Bad idea*, he thought. The room was very nice, and the price was decent. He already loved this holiday. He suddenly felt fresh.

"Let's not waste any time in this room. I hope you're not hungry or tired yet. I've missed the sun, the sea, and this smell. I've missed wearing shorts, T-shirts, and flip-flops," Lewis said.

"Calm down. This isn't London. We're here for change. I don't want you to behave the same way you do over there. No flirting with other girls, no smoking shit, and not too much alcohol. Respect that."

"Come on! Are you jealous?"

"I'm not jealous. Can't you take a break and look at things other than boobs and asses? This holiday is more spiritual. It's for our mental health, for our friendship. I don't want to stay alone while you flirt with your whores."

"Here you go. Why don't you find a man as well?"

"Lewis! You know I'm not interested in that. It's the only thing I'm asking of you. Don't you like change?"

"This is already a big change. Don't misinterpret me when I talk about change. I'm not asking you to change who you are, your nature. Change can be anything, and here we have plenty. The weather has changed, as have the location, the culture, and the cuisine. We're in Sardinia! Let's experience the moment the way we are."

"You'd better not. Otherwise, we meet up here next week for departure."

"Okay! Let's not talk nonsense. Let's start our holiday in peace."

He smiled. They changed and went out for a walk in this new country. The sand was hot, colorful, and shiny. The sea was quiet, blue, and not very busy. A few people swam by the shore. Two or three boats could be seen at the horizon and three Jet Skis raced at a distance.

Her words were like a whirlwind devastating the cells of his body. They kept repeating in his mind. He resigned to grant her wish. He couldn't find pleasure in flirting with others anyway. He wanted to be with her, by her side only. She'd put all of her efforts in making that trip happen. He smiled. He looked at her face and noticed sadness covering her vision. He grabbed her hand and squeezed his fingers between hers without saying a word.

They walked by the seaside, their feet in the water. It felt warm and fresh.

Aylin said, "I've got something to tell you."

"Of course," he responded, full of impatience and surprise.

"I'm confused. My parents want me to go back to my country. I can't stay alone that far from my parents. I can't handle it anymore. I might go back in six months."

"No way! What's your problem? I don't get you. You've been in London for a long time now, far away from everyone. You want to be in London. You've always wanted to be here."

"Yes, but it's hard to convince my parents. They want me to get a job at home. And my student visa will expire soon."

"I'm sure you can find a way to convince them. It's about what *you* want, after all. It's *your* future, not theirs."

"You know the old-fashioned mentality. I have a few exams left, and then I'll be gone."

The world had turned upside down for Lewis. He lost control of his heartbeat. Maybe it wasn't the right time to hear this news. He wished she'd told him that at the end of the trip.

"There's always a way …" Lewis said.

"A way back home," she added.

"A way back home … a way back home … a way back home …"

If only I had a home, he thought, *this girl might stay with me. I'd simply need to show her how much I care about her. She's leaving because her home is far away, and she has to go there; it's calling her. She's leaving because she couldn't find a man in London who could give her a new home. I'm not man enough. I haven't got a home in London, and my home back where I grew up is bitter. I already feel like a foreigner there. Why would I go back again to the escape of my life? I miss her already. I don't want her to go. How can I do it? I can't make her stay. I have no right of staying there myself. What am I going to do?*

"What are you thinking about?" she asked.

"I thought we already discussed this subject?"

"Fuck you."

"I was actually thinking about what we could do this evening." He tried to change the subject and had a classy restaurant in mind. "Let's show some elegance tonight." He smiled.

"Sounds good." She smiled and looked at the horizon.

They walked for hours, their hands fused together. He splashed water on her face. He ran away and she followed him. She jumped on his back, and they both fell on the sand with laughter. He carried her on his back and almost threw her in the sea. She was shouting and begging him to stop, so he did. He softly put her down on the ground and lay next to her. They were both breathless, laughing and giggling.

Time flew by very fast. They headed back to the hotel. Lewis booked a table in a cozy restaurant while Aylin took a shower. They both got dressed after a small nap. Nothing seemed to bother either of them. Lewis forgot about his visa issues, and Aylin forgot about returning to her hometown. Everything was smooth and perfect. His black suit was shiny, his red tie matching her long and tight linen dress. The weather couldn't be better. They could feel the warm wind coming from the hot deserts of Africa. She held his arm, he stopped a taxi, and they made it on time. They hadn't expected the bohemian, shabby, chic decor.

"It's amazing," Aylin said.

They got a table next to the window overlooking a huge swimming pool full of people. Lewis sighed. "There's always a better life. But I guess people living here are bored of it all. They seek to travel somewhere else for the bloody change. This is to say, taking a holiday is the best thing a man can do to enjoy the pleasures of life. There's a whole different culture here—the people, the music, and the food. And of course the weather. It's just perfect. Honestly, this couldn't be this enjoyable without you." He smiled.

Aylin blushed and smiled back. "You'd be in a bar drinking like fish. You'd be barking like a dog at any woman getting close to you. Like a pig, you'd be sniffing around and smoking shit until you'd no longer be yourself. I wanted you to come here. I wanted you to realize that life has more important things in store than those stupidities you're involved in."

"I agree with you. I guess I had no choice."

"What do you mean you had no choice? Have you looked around you? No, you haven't. You ignore the things that are offered to you. You've given up on yourself. Where is your ambition? Where are your goals? Where is your power?"

"I have none."

"You see?"

"Aylin, I'm more than happy to discuss this with you, but not today. This is such a beautiful place. Your red dress illuminates this restaurant. Your presence makes this place busier. I want to live this moment by forgetting what I've been through and ignoring what's coming next. I'm aware of everything. I'm probably a weak person."

"No, you're not. You're the one who's made me stronger. You've helped me find my way."

"It was my duty. I couldn't see you suffer. You deserve many things. Your heart is as pure as clean water."

"What are you planning to do?" Aylin asked. "Your visa expires very soon."

"I don't know. I probably need to get married, but I don't want to."

"But you have to if you don't want to go back to your country."

"Thanks for reminding me."

"You're welcome," she answered sarcastically.

"I'll let time do everything."

"Lewis! Time won't do anything for you. Most of the decisions are in your hands. Go get a better job to support yourself. Go enroll at any university for your doctorate. Do something. There isn't only marriage. What about the entrepreneur visa?"

"I've studied every possibility. In any case, all of them will bring me to the point where I'll have to get married. This idea kills me. I have no other ways. Some more wine?"

"Just a little bit."

Other than the subject they were discussing, the feeling was magical. Nothing could be better. Fresh seafood on the table, a 2006 French white wine, candles lit everywhere, and music enveloping them into another world. They finished eating and decided to go to the swimming pool. There was a party, with people dancing to a live orchestra.

He invited her to dance. They moved around in slow motion, in a way he never danced with anyone else. She was smiling, and the world behind her was smiling. At that point, who cared about the day before, or even the day after? Again questions invaded his body. He struggled, trying to disregard them. Song after song, they both couldn't stop dancing. Aylin was wearing high heels. Her feet were starting to hurt, so they decided to take a break.

"Take off your shoes, and let's go for a walk next to the other swimming pool. It's quieter there."

The stars were shining, and the moon was bigger than ever. It was so close and bright, trying to match Aylin's face. They could hear the waves on the beach. They could hear music everywhere. It was the walk to heaven he'd hoped for.

"This water looks so clean," Aylin said.

"Very tempting," he replied.

Lewis walked close to the edge of the swimming-pool. He pretended to slip and fall in. Aylin screamed and then laughed when she saw him resurfacing.

"Ha-ha, oh, my God. My suit!" Lewis exclaimed. He swam back to the edge. "Oh, God! Help me, please! Your hand," he said. As soon as she reached for his hand, he said, "Sorry!" and pulled her in with a wink.

She screamed, "No!" and splashed into the water. "Asshole! You're an asshole! My dress—it's the first time I'm wearing it!"

"Ha-ha, come here! Please don't hit me. Come here now. It looks much better on you like this. Your hair looks better when it's curly. Don't worry about the dress. I'm sure you'll always remember this one, a special one."

"I already have so many things I'll remember you by."

"Really? Like what?"

"Your stupidity."

"Very funny."

They took off their clothes and put them on the edge. Like mermaids, they danced and sang in the water. They raced and played games, and their hands never drew apart. He felt the warmth of her body against his. Temptation took power like a devil pointing his trident at his victim. Lewis didn't let it overtake him. He fought for her and decided not to. He didn't want to. He thought he loved her too much to make her suffer.

They spent a time, a priceless time, until it was very late. It was an unforgettable evening. Nothing else was involved but their feelings—two bodies and two reasonable brains, careful and stupid. They'd thought too much about the pain to come and forgotten about the amazing moments they were missing every day. They gathered all their clothes and headed back to the hotel room. They were both exhausted. They'd had a long day, but an amazing time. They showered and had ice cream. They lay on the bed and talked until the words took them to the world of dreams.

In the morning, Lewis opened his eyes first. Aylin was sleeping on his chest. His arm was around her neck. He didn't want to wake her up. He remained silent until she woke up.

"Good morning. Did you sleep well?" Lewis asked.

"Yes. You?"

"I fell asleep so quickly. It was a peaceful night."

"What's the plan?"

"Go get a nice tan at the beach?"

"Great!"

Time seemed to fly by faster and faster. Lewis jumped out of his bed, took a quick shower, and already had his towel on his shoulder. They headed to the beach, put on some sunscreen, and lay down underneath the hot, burning sun. A few girls arrived, set up a volleyball net, and started playing. They looked pretty hot.

"They're good! Did you see that?" Lewis said.

"Yes, I saw the pairs of boobs. You're not going anywhere. You're staying here."

"Come on! I didn't mean that."

"No volleyball for you today."

"I'm going for a swim. Be back soon."

It didn't really matter to him. The girls could be hot, but Lewis's intention was simply to be part of the fun. It looked very interesting and fun. Then he thought it wasn't worth it after all, so a swim in the sea would be the thing to make him feel better.

Aylin lay on a towel, reading *The Road Less Traveled.* It was a road not many people walked on, and those who walked on it were blind. It was the course of a life people should have meant to be leading. A lot of reason and wisdom was implemented in the book, a lot of love to be given and shared.

The complication was just human's weakness. She forgot about the sun and the sea. The book took her to a different world. Lewis loved to use that expression: a different world. Everyone had her own world, after all. Aylin's concern was to learn more about her feelings, about her struggle in life. She had almost everything she could have asked for. She was unfortunate, even though (or because) everyone wanted her, Everyone hit on her everywhere and anytime. Her beauty could be seen from a distance, coming out from the very core of her body. Her smile was like a sun that never moved from the centre of the sky. It was so warm and shiny. It never hurt anybody, everybody loved it, and everyone wanted to possess it. She decided to remain above the sky, watching who could be the one who could be the darkness she needed to enlighten. She wasn't looking for a bright light, she wasn't looking for stars, and she wasn't looking for angels or warriors or princes. She was looking for a soul to inhabit her body. She was looking for a man who could get through her burning chest and change the way her heart beat. She couldn't say yes to just anyone. It was not because she had a choice. The truth was she never found any to choose from. Her heart remained cold, saddened by the loneliness of the world. Only Lewis could see the tears of her desires, and only he could feel the shivers of her skin. No matter what, her smile preceded any judgment or interpretation. The way she looked was already enough for a man to tremble in front of her, enough for a man to accept being her slave. The depth of her heart was unknown to people, always misleading. She never rejected people; she allowed them to be around her and called them friends, best friends.

Lewis was a best friend. He wished to last as one, regardless of how much he cared about her, regardless of how much he loved her. That was a secret, and it needed to stay a secret, otherwise that beauty he had with him, that heart he carried next to his, would have been just a dream one told one's friends about the next day. *It's for you, Aylin, that I do this.* Do what? He didn't do anything apart from hiding the truth. He didn't do anything apart from lying to her.

The water was warm and calm. He didn't realize how far he'd swum until he felt the water grow colder than before, and his body tired. He turned around and couldn't see Aylin on the beach anymore; it was too far away. Everything looked so small. It was scary. It was just him and the sea. He could hear only the sound of waves. The sky was blue, and the water was blue. A perfect place to die. Drowning! That could be his last sight, his last breath, his last moment. Aylin could be the last person he'd seen. Death wasn't his worst enemy. He'd welcome it many times, for many reasons.

He finally managed to get back to the beach. He fell on the sand, where the waves were coming up. He closed his eyes, and Aylin appeared in front of him. He realized how important a person could be in someone's life, could change everything, even the way he thought.

"Are you okay? You've been quite far out, as stupid as always."

His head was still in the sand, he breathed heavily, and his heart rate was very high. He couldn't make move. Well, actually, he didn't want to move. It was great to finally be touching the ground again.

"I need to stop smoking. Oh, God. I was nearly there."

"Asshole!"

"I was just testing the value of life. To be honest, I was not in rush to be back on the beach."

"You're starting again!"

"I'm fine. Just a bit tired. I pushed myself a little bit too hard. It's not something I do all the time."

"Taking risks? Yes, it is."

"No, I'm talking about swimming."

He got up from the ground and walked to where they were sitting. Like a piece of cloth, he fell down. He kindly asked Aylin to apply sunscreen on his back. She didn't hesitate for a second. No matter how angry she got, she never resented him in the slightest. It was as if all he did was right. Her hands rubbed all over his back, his feet, and even his head. Words couldn't say it better. Every touch was a miraculous song. He felt her hands caressing his heart and her soul penetrating his body. His eyes were closed. There was nothing to see. Nothing could be said at all.

He opened his eyes as soon as she stopped applying the cream. She'd probably taken only a minute for the whole thing, but it had felt like she'd spent the whole day massaging his back. He hated the situation. His tongue was moving, about to spit out something inappropriate, but he stopped it for some reason. *Let's not ruin the moment*, he thought. He pretended to have fallen asleep.

They spent almost all day on the beach. They had some sandwiches and drank some margaritas. The place did not really make any difference. Lewis always enjoyed spending time with Aylin. Wherever they'd been, whatever they'd eaten or drunk, it had always been a moment of joy and relaxation. The beautiful time had taken them back to the hotel. They got ready to go out. That time was a time of improvisation. There were no plans for the night. They simply had to follow their steps to somewhere cool.

They walked to an Asian restaurant and had some roast pork and rice. They had two glasses of wine and left. Both were attracted by the wind coming from the sea, and they decided to walk along the beach. They heard some music and then perceived some people around a huge fireplace in the middle of the beach.

"That's pretty cool," Lewis said. "Let's check out what they're doing."

"Are you sure fire is allowed on a public beach?"

"Allowed? It doesn't look like they just set it. Can't you see how many people are around it? The police wouldn't arrest that many. Look how wonderful things can be. Easy life. It costs the happiness of the world. The things we have to pay for, the things we dream of every day—here, they're offered, they're shared. The warmth of the universe isn't enough. They lit a fire to unite them in one place. Everyone's buying beer, and some are stewing ribs. There are two guitars and three different drummers. This is what I call a beautiful moment. Everyone's singing at the same time. A choral I've never heard before, so spontaneous, so unplanned, so smooth and perfectly performed."

"I see."

Lewis and Aylin didn't say a word once they sat down with the crowd. They were laughing as they looked at each other and then around them. They remained there to enjoy every single note, every voice that matched the rhythm. The light of the fire embraced every face. Smiles were everywhere, and people were standing, sitting, dancing, and singing. Aylin grabbed Lewis's hand and leaned on his shoulder. He put his arm around her neck and kissed her on the forehead. A few hours went past very quickly.

"Shall we go?" she said.

"I really enjoy it here, but I guess we can do whatever you want."

When they were hand in hand, time didn't have any value. Whether it was the way back to the hotel or to somewhere else, whether it was the time to die or to have an eternal life, nothing really bothered their minds. That moment was a moment of revelation. But no revelation was made. Silence always spoke more than words ever could. They got into the hotel room, fell on the bed together, and fell asleep.

Neither of them wanted to go back to London. Neither of them wanted to work. Neither of them wanted to change anything. Sweet mornings seasoned with her sweet face, so bright on a white pillow. The sunbeam woke him up because the curtains weren't closed. Lewis couldn't move, but he didn't want to move. Once again he wished he could stay there forever, watching her sleep.

The morning went quickly. The day flew by even quicker as they enjoyed shopping and meeting new people. Someone invited them to a club—the best one around, they were told. Aylin hesitated, but Lewis was up for it. He managed to convince her to join them, and they were supposed to meet at 11:00 p.m.

"The beach party! Mmm, I'll rock it tonight. Aren't you excited?"

"You know clubs are not really my thing."

"I know, but this is different. It's not London."

"I perfectly know that."

Sure, it wasn't London, but Lewis had always been Lewis.

The moment they got in, Lewis started having shots with his new friends, three guys and three girls. He danced and drank like it was the first time in his life. Aylin had one glass of wine as usual. She sat down at a table and watched him go crazy. She remembered all those times she'd had to see him drink away his pain and flirt with other girls. She remembered every girl he'd spoken to, every girl he'd kissed, every time he'd made her heart cry. That day, she gathered all her pain—the ones of that day and the ones she'd experienced times ago because of him because of her feelings for him. She held her breath and remained silent.

"Hey! Come to dance. Come on!" Lewis said.

He pulled her hand and dragged her with him to the dance floor. She danced a few minutes and went back to her seat. Lewis didn't persist because he knew her way.

Aylin was a classy girl. She sometimes went out to nightclubs for the sake of going out with her friends. She'd rather go to a bar where she could relax and talk. Loud music and unnecessary moves were never her cup of tea. She'd sit down and watch people around her, or she'd check her phone every minute. She'd also always have one eye on Lewis.

She noticed that he was going to the bathroom every ten to twenty minutes. Of course, the more he drank, the more he needed to empty his bladder. But was it really the only thing that took him to the bathroom so often? While Lewis was on the dance floor, flirting with one of those girls, one of the guys came to see Aylin. He invited her for a drink, which she rejected, and then he asked her if, like Lewis, she'd like to take some cocaine. Furious, she stood up, grabbed her bag, and made her way to the exit.

Lewis, surprised, saw her reaction from the dance floor and followed her. "Aylin! Aylin, wait! Wait!"

He managed to catch her by the arm. She turned around and slapped him in the face in the middle of the crowd. It felt as if the whole club had stopped dancing and was looking at him.

"You're an asshole, Lewis! You cannot change, not even for a few days. You'll never change. I was hoping. I thought you would, and you promised. It's the only thing I asked you not to do on this little holiday. Leave me alone. Go away!"

"Wait! What's your problem?"

"My problem? Do you think I'm stupid? You've drunk more than you've ever done, you don't stop sniffing that shit, and then you rub your cock on those whores *in front of me*. Again and again, nonstop! I can't deal with this anymore, Lewis. You've pushed me too far away from you."

She left, devastated. It was as if she held her heart between her hands, her tears floating through the air. She cried loudly, and he could hear her from a distance. At that moment, many things crossed his mind. All those things he'd done in front of her had been to push her away from him. Then he listened to his heartbeat. What if he was about to lose her forever?

He ran after her, calling her name everywhere. She couldn't have gone to the hotel room; it wasn't the right direction. He walked and searched in every alley of the area. He followed a small pathway leading to the beach and then saw her sat down on the sand.

"Aylin, I'm really sorry. Since we've gotten to this point, I think I have something important to tell you. You should know that what you're going to hear might hurt you even more."

She was motionless. He couldn't even hear her cry anymore. He paused for a few minutes and then went on.

"It's been years since the day we first met. Ever since that day, you've been so special to me. You have always enlightened my way. You make my days brighter every time I see you. I've had the chance to take a look at inside of your heart. I've been trapped and have fallen in love with you. Maybe you've been crying, but you've not been the only one. I was and am crying for the things I did in front of you. Yes, it was to push you away from me, because I never wanted you to be hurt. I thought you deserved more, better than me. And you really do. My future isn't certain. I cannot decide, and I am irresponsible. I thought I'd rather be your friend than a lover who would let you down in the end. I've never wanted to treat you the same way I treated all those girls I met.

"I've always looked at you as the perfect girlfriend. I've always wished to have you by my side, to finally kiss you the way I've always desired to, to gather all my passion in one powerful hug and give it to you. I've been living in a lie all this time in a way I've never experienced in my life before. You know, I might end up going back to Algeria, and the only way for me to stay in England is to get married. Both would hurt you more than anything. So I've had to make sure you believe we're friends. This is the biggest challenge for me, knowing that there is no such a thing as friendship between a man and a woman."

He paused.

"I haven't run out of words yet. I love you. I've loved you all the way for who you are. And I guess I've shown you my real me. I couldn't be fake with you. Yes, I do like women. Yes, I do take drugs for my own reasons. Yes, I do drink alcohol; it has become a necessity. That is all me. But I do care about you. I do ask after you. I secretly gave you my heart and every hope I have. I've never wished for things to be this way. Besides, you also have to go back to your country. You depend on your parents. I have no choice. This is my fate, Aylin. This is probably the biggest sacrifice I've ever made: my love for your comfort. I'm sorry. I'm really sorry."

He paused once more while tears ran down his face. Then he added, "I think I've said enough for today. I'll see you at the hotel."

"Wait! Please don't go," she said.

He stopped without turning around. He didn't want her to see him cry. "I'll see you inside. I really need some space now," he said.

"I love you too. I do. You're the cause of all my tears. Yes, I'm hurt because I'm scared, I'm confused, I'm lost. I don't know who you are and what you want. I'm living in a dream—a dream you've broken."

"Aylin! Please. I think we should cry on our own tonight. From this moment on, everything between us will be different. I don't know whether it will be good or bad, but the feeling I get now is very threatening. I'll see you later."

He made his way toward the beach and left Aylin shattered. He could feel her pain because he was in the same pain. He wasn't sure whether the step he was about to take was right. Till that point, he'd never done anything right for her anyway. He pressed his hand against his chest and let his tears flow again, always at the edge. Every word she'd said had been an arrow piercing his heart. Ben was right: He never should have accepted going on this trip. On the other hand, he'd been looking forward to those words from her. He'd been looking forward to revealing his feelings to her. It had happened in an unexpected way. He wished he'd been ready for it. He wished he was free to decide. He wished he was that son of the universe to choose where to live or when to leave.

Algeria, his worst nightmare. He hated his country, he hated his origins, and he hated his life in general. How could he bear the thought of going back? How could he bear the thought of losing Aylin? The world was blank, and so was his soul. Only pain filled up his body. He spent hours thinking about what to do and how to face her again. She was not only his best friend. She was everything to him. She was the faith he'd always wanted to have, a forbidden one.

He bent down to take some water from the sea. As soon as he touched it, images of Algeria appeared in front of him. A connection between the two continents. The free man and the slave. Slaves of life. He'd seen a fence; he'd seen walls, tall ones blocking his sight. Faraway in a dry desert. He'd seen injustice and tasted the bitterness of the land as he washed his face. The water woke him up like a morning after a bad dream. It was so intense, so real.

The other truth was Aylin was either crying in the same place where he'd left her or sleeping on the bed he was supposed to share with her. He couldn't stay out all night; the moment of loneliness had come to its end. Aylin was awaiting him.

The room was dark, and Aylin was sleeping. He noticed a few tissues on the floor. She'd cried enough. He got into bed, underneath the sheet. He tried not to move, lying on his back and facing the ceiling. He wished things were different. Hold on—they actually were. He'd never expected that to happen. He remembered the first time he'd gotten in bed with her. It had felt the same. It was the first time they both went out together. They used to meet up in a bar where he used to work. She was the best customer he'd ever had, and her face had never left his mind. Every time she walked in was a rebirth. She changed the whole atmosphere, making it peaceful and calm.

The time she invited him out after work had been the most amazing surprise. When did he ever act that way? He remained next to her, drank wisely, and made sure he wasn't hitting on other girls. He didn't flirt with her; he didn't try to. That girl certainly was different. When she felt tired and a bit drunk, she said she was just tipsy and wanted to go to the Chelsea Bridge to see the lights. She wanted to feel the freezing cold wind and pray under the stars. There were no stars; it was cloudy, and she was drunk. He convinced her to go home, and she asked him if he could drop her off. When they got there, she begged him to stay over. He thought it would be wiser. He was also tired and needed to work the next day.

They got in bed, and he held her in his arms and tried to sleep. He couldn't close his eyes. He couldn't move either. He'd felt her warmth flowing around his body. He watched the ceiling for the rest of the night until he finally fell asleep.

When he woke up in the hotel room, Aylin wasn't in bed. He felt tired and lazy. It had been a harsh, emotional night. He called her name, but there was no answer. She wasn't in the shower either.

I need to fix this.

She could be anywhere. Having lunch on her own, or lying down on the sand. She could be shopping; spending money helped to reduce stress. Loneliness was never bad. She could be thinking about the previous night; she could be trying to forget. The worst would be heading to the airport and leaving him behind. He wasn't worth going abroad with. He was worth neither the effort nor the energy, and he knew that.

He'd never wanted her to go through all of that, but all he did was hurt her again and again. He needed to fix the situation.

Yes, it was a must, but he also knew that the situation was most likely unsolvable. No matter how beautiful everything could have been, he'd still have to leave the country—in other words, leave Aylin behind. And Aylin was not just any girl. It was a double pain for him. The pain of having no choice, and the pain of hurting the one person who didn't deserve to be hurt. She didn't deserve to be misled. She didn't deserve to be betrayed or punished. The punishment of love was like a curse on both of them.

He made an effort and got up from his bed. He washed his face and went to find Aylin. She was by the swimming pool. The atmosphere wasn't at its best, but he was happy to have found her easily. He bought a drink and went to sit down next to her. He found it hard to say good morning. She didn't hear him; only a whisper had come out of his mouth. A couple of hours passed under the strong sun. Neither said anything. Both had their mouths zipped. The lack of courage prevented them from uttering the first words. Lewis actually didn't want to talk at all. The whole moment of silence was broken only by occasional splashes in the water, people screaming, planes flying above, and music from every direction. Aylin, at last too irritated on her sun bed, removed her sunglasses and opened her mouth.

"We need to talk," she said.

"Yes, we should, but I wonder what's right to say."

"I don't care about right or wrong. I want to understand. I want to hear you talk. I want you to open your ears and listen to me too."

"Aylin, I'm sorry about yesterday. I shouldn't have acted that way. I'm just used to it. I did drink a lot, and I did take some drugs. I broke my promise and made you suffer. I'm sorry. I don't know what to do with my life, and this is it. I've lost control of reason. I no longer recognize myself in the mirror."

Aylin burst into tears. He thought maybe it would be better to stop talking. He watched her crumble. He watched her suffer! *She's suffering. She's crying. She's in pain. Because of me!* He couldn't say a word. He remained silent for a moment but then decided to speak up.

"Let me be honest. Most of my life has been a pain in the ass. Somehow, I chose to be so because I couldn't do anything else. My friends called me unstable, and others called me a playboy. Unstable seems to summarize it perfectly. It's true I never found my path. Playboy? Okay, I'm constantly surrounded by women, and I hit on any beautiful mortal I see passing by. In the past, it was a quest to find love. I kept changing my partners in order to find the right one. Lately, I don't know anymore. Things are so different. I just go for fun. I do it for the sake of not being alone.

"My heart, all of it, belonged to you from the start. Now you know the main reason I didn't show you my flames. I couldn't say a word in front of you. I tried to express myself while we were together and alone in my own world. I have so many things on my mind. The difficulty in moving forward resides in my restrictions. I found words for every girl I met, but all of them were purely sexual. This speech to you is more emotional, deeper. It's coming from the deepest parts of my heart, and my words can be confused.

"This is one of the nicest places I've ever been to. It's caused the awakening of my internal volcano spitting unwanted reactions. I expected as much, and all I did was try to avoid it. I'm losing control of myself. We could have stopped everything before it actually came to where we are now, but we didn't want to stop it. We wanted it to happen.

"Why would I feel guilty for something we've beautifully felt? Guilt is evil. There's no guilt here; there's no regret now that I've told you the way I feel. I just wish you'd have known this from the beginning that I'd shown you what you really meant to me. By trying to protect you, I've destroyed you. Everything has consequences. I hadn't considered this one. I thought our feelings would quickly disappear, and then I could watch you, happy to be your friend. The sacrifice would be to see you happy with someone else, and I thought I'd never be able to do that. My heart went crazy when I heard you say your parents want you to go back home. I realized at that I was at the edge of losing you. I've already experienced the feeling of you being far away, but you always came back. Your presence is the light during my dark days. Knowing you're close to me geographically is already a relief. I've always argued with you for not being in a constant touch with me because I needed you, I needed to hear your voice. The way I desired it was not just the love of close friendship. It was obviously different. I tried to convince myself by putting my hurts first instead of yours. You've tried to be with some people, to find love. I was happy and ready to help you, but my heart was in the worst circumstances, not even able to breathe at the idea of you being with someone else. My heart wants you more than anything, and all it did was reject every single person trying to come into my life. I was a liar; lying to you and lying to myself.

"I'm losing my mind, but my eyes are open. I ask you not to make any sacrifices. Life creates restrictions so someone can break them down. I don't know if we can do it. Do you think it's worth trying? We're so close to the end of our journey in the United Kingdom. How can we do it?

"Please forgive me. I'm not perfect, nothing is perfect, but this is beautiful. We've been honest with each other at last. We're both special to each other. This will remain forever, no matter what. But again, how?"

Sardinia felt like it had risen from the ground and was floating on the tears they both shed. They couldn't look into each other's eyes. They both looked deep into their hearts. Aylin had something to say. Lewis remained silent until she finally opened her mouth. Her lips were trembling.

"I never thought I'd hear you say something like that. Neither did I think I'd ever say a word in front of you. After what happened yesterday in that club, I felt as if I'd already given up on us, but I haven't. I just don't want to! On the other hand, I don't know what to do anymore. I really don't. I'm ready to wait patiently to see where all this is going. If only I had a little hope, that would help a lot. I feel like I'm letting something important in my life go away, something I just found, something that makes me happy and makes me forget about everything else.

"You know, I actually didn't believe that one day I could feel this way. I thought I'd lost my hope and belief a long time ago. After my break-up with Oscar, I thought my feelings had died when he left. I buried my feelings deep inside and I was scared to let them out again. I was convinced I wouldn't be able to take it anymore. For years, I felt like I was broken into tiny pieces. How many times have I tried to stick them all together? Every time, it got worse and worse. So after my last relationship, I promised I wouldn't fall in love again, wouldn't let anyone hurt me ever again, wouldn't let my feelings take me over. I was wrong, I guess—a heart that feels has no brain that reasons. All those times, I was trying not to fall into your trap. I ended up believing that with you, I cannot control it anymore. I hate it on the one hand, but on the other, I experienced something magical. Thanks to you, if before I was just existing, now I feel alive. I have so much going on inside of me that I can't even describe with words.

"Yesterday, when you left, I reviewed all those moments we've spent together in my mind. I froze on every dance we've danced, every meal we've had, every laugh we've shared. I looked so happy! You make me happy, and I'm so grateful for that. I really am! I just wish I realized it earlier. I think I actually did realize it, but I was lying to myself because you weren't mine. I wasn't sure about your feelings. I was so confused and couldn't figure it out. And when I didn't see a move from your side,

I was convinced I was just a friend of yours. I wish we'd had the courage to disclose it earlier to each other. And now, when I think of it, it hurts me even more. I had the best years with our friendship. I wish it had been more than that. Now that I'm about to lose you, I realize how important you are in my life. I don't know if I can imagine myself without you. I swear I tried, but it's just not working. I'm too attached to you, now more than ever. I stayed in London for a reason. I wanted something to happen. Better late than never.

"I feel so weird inside, as if something very heavy is pulling me down. I want to let it out; I want to tell you more. It seems almost impossible, but it's happening. I can keep on talking incessantly. I can keep on saying how much you mean to me, how far we could go together.

"I just hope you'll get your visa without going through all this trouble with marriage. I want to believe in us so we won't need to go through hell, so we won't have to be apart. I love you. Come here, please."

Happiness! Was it happiness he felt when his heart wanted to scream? He was in the middle of the ocean; only water surrounded his existence. The waves were calm but then became violent. He wanted to drown himself. A suicide was never a bad idea. He couldn't believe what he'd said, not what he'd heard.

In front of him on a sun bed was the most amazing woman he had ever met. Her arms were wide open, welcoming him to share her dazzling warmth. His body moved as his tears fell down. The hug of life, the hug of his own devastation. It wasn't just happiness; his sorrow had a hold of his hand. He couldn't be the person enjoying the present anymore. He was with a woman he'd think about tomorrow, finding a solution for something he'd never be able to solve. He had no power.

He leaned on her chest, closed his eyes, and tried to understand the emotional reaction caused by his words and by her words. He got into a gloomy forest that welcomed him in and invited him to see its best flowers. The flowers of life would help him find his way to his grave. It wasn't a betrayal; it was the normal course of life itself.

He wanted to stop thinking. He leaned on a golden chest. She was there, and finally they both knew what they felt for each other. That was the tree of life, the tree of pure knowledge.

The whole world meant nothing at that moment. Trees, skies, oceans, gods—they all disappeared from his mind, the empty life, a lonely star in an endless space.

His head was on her chest, nothing like it was the first time. Things became different. Her perfume, her sweat, her heartbeat, the softness of her skin, and her long hair around her shoulders. It was a safe place, a tender and weak place. He didn't want to move—why would he?

She held him tighter. He felt comfort, and he felt as if his body was part of hers.

"Lewis, I love you. I've loved you from day one."

"I love you too," he replied with a shaky voice. "Can we just stay like this? Please?"

"Of course," she replied.

They spent all afternoon entangled under the hot sun. Nothing could be as warm as the beat of their hearts. He felt the need to die. Love could lead to despair, but nothing in life could be better than the comfort of her love—that was life itself. His weakness gave that moment the desire to take away his life. He wanted to close his eyes and never open them again. Because he knew what was going to happen next; he could predict it. He'd had a premonition. Confusion invaded his body. But at that point, all his heart had to accept was to stay next to her.

Let it be.

The rest of the holiday was certainly different. They could finally see each other's real faces and real smiles. Dinners were more succulent, drinks were fresher, the sun was hotter, and their hearts were warmer. They walked hand in hand, had kisses on the sand, and had fights in the water. It took them to bed. Bed was not just a bed, and it was not a nest to lay in eggs. It couldn't be called having sex—it was the discovery of making love.

He couldn't describe it the way he'd easily done with other girls. He couldn't think of it that way. He couldn't imagine himself writing down the experience. He couldn't confess the delicacy of her touch, the sweetness of her lips, the softness of her skin. If he could ever write something about this experience, it would be on the board of his heart. The confession would be to the pastor of his soul residing in the depth of his body.

Happy moments brought them back to London, and they stayed at her place all the time. He started looking for a job and thought about drinking and smoking less, but that never happened. It was hard to find a decent job; it was hard to find a solution for his visa issues. She made his life harder as time ran out. Ben was pushing him to get married. His friend had some reason left in his brain, whereas Lewis was in love and could never accept that option.

Aylin became the main dream of his reality. He wanted to achieve so much. She gave him the courage, she gave him the strength, and she gave him everything he needed.

He tended to forget his worries. So did Aylin.

Chapter 11

"Nothing is really surprising in life."

"Please, all I want is to be with you. I don't want to think about tomorrow. I don't care what will happen tomorrow. I might lose you, so please be here with me now. I want to make the most out of it," she said.

He saw himself gliding in the air, fulfilled with happiness and comfort. He saw himself eating in restaurants, going to the cinema, drinking in bars, chilling at home, and making love to the woman who made him believe in himself, the woman who'd woken up his latent emotions, the woman who'd changed the way his heart beat. The magical world existed. His heart grew bigger; he finally managed to start liking the world around him. People didn't bother him anymore. He smiled during the day and slept peacefully at night. He ate properly and started rereading a few books he'd left on the side a while ago.

The girl next to him was the source of his ambition. She fed his emotions, caressed his heart, and wrapped it in a woolen box to keep it warm all the time. Nothing could be more beautiful than what he felt.

Who could have believed a person—just a normal person, a human being—could change someone's life in no time? The empty body was filled with a presence. A constant traffic of emotions and hope ran throughout all of his existence.

He spoke to Ben only over the phone. He didn't get much time to go out and see him.

"Lewis, I have to see you. Come on! You're an asshole. Now you're in love, so you've completely forgotten about me?"

"Ben! Please, not you. No pressure. The Future—meet me there at six this evening."

"I finish work at six. Make it seven."

"All right, see you later."

Seeing Ben was not the easiest thing, and neither was it the wisest. Lewis perfectly understood the course of his circumstances. But he did miss him, and seeing him would make him very happy. His jokes, his laughter, his behavior—everything about him was amazing.

He wandered home, had a drink, and then left, smoking his first joint of the day on his way there. He got to the Future quite early and waited for Ben to show up.

Was there any world around without girls and temptation? Was there in each of those worlds any man who could escape that temptation, that strange desire of female attraction? They were everywhere. The only thing that could keep a person away from all of them was the respect he had for his lover. Sacrifice all those beauties and kill all those emotions for the sake of a better one, the best one. The one who was present even when she was absent.

He looked down and watched his beer. He saw a lot of bubbles. Every bubble was a life. It started somewhere in the bottom or in the middle and died on the top. A very short life. All of them together gave that beer what those girls gave to a man: desires that made his own life the richest. All those bubbles were part of the refreshing taste of that beer, just like those girls refreshing the emotions of a man's existence. *Unfortunately, we humans have the vice of possessiveness, and only one bubble should belong to one person.*

It was a huge commitment, giving up all the others for only one person, but that person was Aylin. He had to close his eyes and never look again at any of them. He had to see her on every face so that the feeling of guilt would precede any desire or attraction. His heart was in war against his reason, a restricted love that put boundaries to his freedom.

A beer, just a beer, became the theme of his thoughts, comparing it to a life in which he regrettably had to live. He forgot about the world around him. He waited for Ben, who was as late as always. He finally showed his face at the bar, hiding the joy of finally seeing Lewis after a couple of months. Phone calls were never enough; not seeing each other every single weekend hadn't been easy. Lewis got up, smiled, opened his arms, and hugged his friend.

"Please understand me," Lewis said.

"It's okay. Let's have a beer."

They ordered a couple of beers and sat down.

"I'm so sorry. I know whatever I tell you will never justify me being so distant, but I guess you're the only one I can open up to. How are you, anyway?" Lewis said.

"I'm good. I haven't been out for quite a while too."

"It's just that someone is changing the way I am, and it makes me feel good."

"You've changed me too, Lewis. I've never been like this before. You're the only one who made me forget about my worries. I started a different life with you. I tend to forget that I don't have a visa, that I could be arrested at any time and be sent back home. Lately, I'm more worried about you, and I don't want you to be in the same shit. You know your relationship with Aylin is a gamble."

"I'm trapped indeed, like the soldiers of Tariq Ibn Ziad. There's no escape. This is love, my friend. I'm very aware of the consequences of this situation. You know, this is what I understood from life. There is nothing better than to enjoy than the happiness we feel in the present time. Tomorrow is never predictable. I might leave Aylin and still go back to Algeria in any case, so I want to live every moment I have with her. I want to feel this way today and not waste my time hoping I'll feel it in the future. She's a very nice girl, and she's experiencing the same feelings. Her heart is so rich, and she's decided to give it all to me. I want to accept it. It might take a month, a year, or an eternity. I don't have time to worry about tomorrow. I don't have time to speculate, predict, and pretend things could happen in a certain way. I do love her. Maybe I hid this feeling from you, but I know I was never good at it. You could see it in my eyes; you asked me several times. I didn't expect the last drop to overflow my body. I fell for it, Ben. My heart isn't with me right now. It's with her. Don't worry. What I have for you will never change, but I need to calm down a little bit. We still can go out, but less often and not at the moment. It's very hectic."

"Is this your current dream?"

"I don't know what my dream is."

"Dreams can give you wings, like the ones you have now. But you should fly where you can easily land, just in case they break down. If you fly higher, the crash could be destructive."

"You speak wisely now." Lewis laughed. "I know what you mean. I won't fly very high. I'll fly high enough to enjoy the sight from the skies. Beauty is from up there."

"You have one month left before your visa expires."

"My visa! And this visa will be of no use if I lose Aylin."

"Remember where you come from. When you were back home, you'd have married a seventy-year-old European woman if it meant leaving the country. You wanted to buy a visa that costs twenty thousand euros. You wanted to commit suicide, and you actually tried because you were fed up. You tried every way to leave the country. You applied for student, tourist, and business visas, and all were rejected. How many countries did you try? You had the chance of a lifetime to come to England, and now you're talking about love. What's love? A feeling that breaks you down one day or another. I've never had a girlfriend because I don't want to be controlled, I don't want to lose my reason. Love! We're not in a situation where we can explore our feelings. Your first priority when you arrived in this country was to get a passport, no matter how, in order to stay here. You're fucking it up for yourself, and the worst part is you know it. Let her be the sacrifice of your future. You'll always find another lover; you'll always be able to have feelings for another person. Who could have thought you could love again after your ex? You were crazy about her. She's gone. This one will go too, and you'll save your life from more miseries. You'll find your freedom, and then once you have a stable situation and have no worries about where to live or stay, then and only then will you enjoy having someone by your side. No restrictions. I know you won't listen to what I say. But as your friend, I urge you to get married first."

"I haven't forgotten my past and I'm fully aware of the current conditions. You're right. On the other hand, I believe happiness is the shortest feeling you could ever feel. I'm happy now. I think I could have been happy back home if I'd found someone like Aylin, if I'd ever loved someone like her. There's a huge difference between my ex and Aylin. They're two different kinds of love. I suddenly fell in love with my ex, and I couldn't control myself. I let myself go like a leaf blown away in the wind. It took me to where agony resides. Throughout the relationship, I knew how incompatible we were, but I couldn't leave. I suffered all the way.

"With Aylin, the restriction itself made me discover who she was. She won my respect first, and only then did it develop into a loving emotion. Time taught me to love her. I still have my reason I could leave and not go back to see her now, but I'd lose this amazing opportunity of being who I really am. I am myself with her. I love the way she's with me, and I love the way I am with her. If only I didn't have this visa problem. I could show her more attention, I could give her more love. I could be the happiest man on Earth because she's amazing. Love is amazing, Ben.

"I've known the secrets of love. To tell you the truth, I'm no longer living on the same Earth as you. We're in two different and complicated dimensions. This might be why you don't find me as reasonable as you are. No one knows what the right reason is, anyway. But mine is to be happy now, just now, while I can feel it. My worry about my visa and Algeria will only spoil the moment, especially if I were to lose her. I know I'm playing a game that I will certainly lose. I simply don't let it interfere with my emotions at the moment. I'm hoping to find a solution very soon. Trust me."

"You've shown me that we should face the truth in this life. You've guided me and advised me, and always in the right way. I'm trying to do the same for you for the first time. I might understand the strength of your attachment to Aylin. I might be able to guess how important she can be in your life. But think twice, Lewis. You're the wisest man I've ever known, although some people thought you were stupid and arrogant. I'll let you sort out this shit. Think about Algeria!"

There were a few words in the language that made Lewis shiver, and one of them was *Algeria*. His memories were the worst he could ever have. He remembered having problems with himself, his own existence. He'd had issues and felt anxiety, stress, and depression, but he never found the source of those disturbing reactions. He remembered all those sad faces, covered faces, intolerance, corruption, extremists … He remembered what couldn't be forgotten. He realized that his pain was worse than any love he'd ever felt. Images appeared in front of him, and there were horrors of Algeria alternating with Aylin's face. There was no explanation to anything. Everything was meant to happen that way.

Ben liked Aylin so much, and he'd have loved to see Lewis and her together. They could make a great couple; everyone had always doubted their friendship. Maybe it was the energy they both spread all around. Ben wasn't thinking about his own situation, even though it must have been worse than Lewis's, but he still felt pity and also guilt for not being able to help his friend, for not being able to grant him at least one wish. Instead, he tried to break up one of his dreams, the one for which he'd always lived.

They drank their beers, and spoke about life and death the whole evening. Lewis thought it was late, so he decided to leave. Ben didn't object and left too.

The worst war a human being might endure was the internal war, the war between what was right and what was wrong, and then both against a third party, emotions. Only a strong person could survive that war. A weak person would lose his mind and fall into depression.

Marriage! The only thing Lewis really wanted to idealize in life was marriage. One might earn enough money; one might not live the perfect life or travel or eat better than buttered bread. But still, he'd always been able to find true love. And true love created the best weddings and unions in existence.

Lewis had always been looking for the ideal one, for the perfect one to make his wedding the best he could dream of—not in terms of how much it cost but how deep his feelings would be for the woman he was to marry. Aylin could potentially be the one, but feelings were not the only elements needed for a couple to merge.

Fuck faith, he thought.

His mind was filled with negative stimuli, which caused him to talk when he got home.

She opened the door, and he saw her smile. Her hug strangled his heart, and then his words faded in his brain. He sat down on the sofa, switched on the TV, and seemed to look at the moving images. His thoughts were regenerating, and this time his mouth couldn't keep the words inside.

"Aylin!" he called.

She answered from the other room and made her way to the living room.

"Sit down, please. We need to talk."

"Sure! Are you okay?"

"Yes, I am. Somehow! You know, I really love this—you and me together. I think this is the best time of my life. You see, things got very complicated. The complication is love. We both know this is going to stop in no time. One month. Let me finish, please," he said as she made a move to talk. "I have no money to register for another course. I keep applying for jobs, but I only get those that aren't remunerated. Because of the current situation on the market, no one actually gets jobs, and how do you expect me to get a sponsorship while those who already have jobs are losing them? I'm so fucked. Only marriage can make me stay here. Without marriage, I'll have to go back to Algeria, which would make our relationship impossible. Or I could stay over here illegally, but again, the same ..."

"What do you mean?"

"I need to find someone who can help me stay here. Someone who can help, who will marry me as a friend. It's the only efficient way of remaining here for certain."

"Are you serious? What about me? Do you think I'm going to wait for you for three to five years?"

"We'll be together all that time. It's not like I'm getting married for real. It will be fake, and then I'll get a divorce as soon as I sort out my documents. It will take at least three years, but it won't affect us in any way. I won't be living with her; we will be living together."

"You know you cannot do that, Lewis. I can't deal with that."

The atmosphere was getting tense, and Lewis lost his temper.

"So what do you want from me?" he shouted. "I'm sure you'd never come to Algeria with me. So all you're waiting for is this month to come to an end? Do you really think once my visa expires, I'd go back to where I came from? That's never going to happen. So either I get married, or I stay here illegally. There is no other way."

"So you're choosing the easiest solution for you to stay here."

"No, Aylin. I'm using the most effective and the only solution. You don't know how hard it is for me to do it. I'm left without any choice. I'll be gone, Aylin. Can you see me leave? Do you think love will work in a long-distance relationship between Algeria and England or your native country? You won't stay here either; your visa will expire right after mine. If I go back to Algeria, that would be suicidal. The moment I set a foot on that ground, I'll shoot a bullet through my head. That is, if I don't find a way of doing it on the plane. I'm done with that hell. And if you take what I say too easily, then let me tell you that thinking of being taken back there is my daily nightmare. It won't happen. I'm left with only one option. How would you take it? If I get married, at least I'd be able to get you to stay with me. We'll live together and then finally move on."

She had her head between her hands. Tears fell on her knees. Those tears were tears of awareness. It wasn't something she'd ignored before; it was something she'd tried to not think about. The moment of truth had come. "I'm sorry! I just can't see you with anybody else. You know how much I love you," she said.

"I know, Aylin. Love isn't the problem here. The problem is how we can stay together. And I won't be with anyone else. It's just documents to sign."

"It's fine, get married. I can't change it."

Lewis had the permission he'd never been given before. He preferred not to talk about it further. He closed the subject by saying, "Sorry. I'll do my best not to have to resort to getting married. I'm still working on getting a work permit. But if I do get married, then please don't get upset. I'll only do it to make sure I'll remain here with you. I love you."

Just a few days were left. There was almost no chance of finding a woman. His heart felt heavy, breathless. The world was turning around his head, he couldn't see anything, and he couldn't hear anything. Life was really unfair to both of them. What a perfect love it could have been! Lewis left her place with these ideas. They thought maybe a little distance could help them get some wisdom, and maybe they'd think of further solutions.

His thoughts took him from one bar to another while Aylin cried her eyes out. Alcohol was not enough, so he smoked and took a few lines of cocaine. Aylin called him, but he wasn't in the best state of mind to answer. He pulled himself out of the club and called a cab to take him home. He didn't have enough cash. His card wasn't working. The taxi driver beat the shit out him and left him on the floor next to his front door. A neighbor helped him stand up. He opened his door, got inside and, fell asleep on the staircase. He cried more and more tears every minute.

The next day, he cleaned himself up. He called Aylin, but she didn't answer. He checked his e-mails and found a message from one of his friends, Anna.

Dear Lewis,

I've read your message a few times, and I've been thinking how harsh life has been to you. I've also been thinking of a way I could help you, and I realize I wouldn't be losing anything. So, why not? I can help. I want to help you.

He phoned the girl immediately. They spoke about everything in detail, and she agreed. They'd do it as soon as possible before his visa expired.

He called Aylin again, but she still didn't answer. He thought about it very carefully and decided not to tell her because she had her last exam to conclude the long years of stressful studies.

He booked a place, organized a party, and invited his closest friends to fake a nice crowd. He told each of them to keep the secret and especially not to mention it to Aylin. Ten days later, on his wedding day, his friends were there, and so were the officers and two witnesses. He stood up in front of that beautiful girl who was making a big commitment just to help him. *Why me?* The officer made sincere statements to which he had to swear. He was talking about true love, union, and eternity. Those words, one by one, were like arrows penetrating every feeling he'd ever had for Aylin. All he heard were words, and all he saw was her face.

He didn't know what to feel; everything was confusing. He had that girl next to him, smiling to everyone. Things looked so real to the outside world. *If only things were this real. My friends are happy, and so is the girl next to me. This is such a risk we're taking. I could lose everything at this precise moment. This could take me anywhere.*

After the ceremony, they went for a drink, ate some food, and took pictures to be included in the application for his stay in the UK.

Around 9:00 p.m., everyone was tired and decided to go home. His wife was drunk, and so were most of his guests. He asked Ben to take care of the girl, his wife, and he ran to knock on Aylin's door. Everything was too much for him. He felt weird and unreal. He had to respect the girl who'd married him. She was the most charitable girl he'd ever met, full of kindness, wisdom, sympathy, and gifts. She was his angel and had come to save him. She'd come to save his soul from the hovering misery. She'd brought him the key to freedom, the key to life and love. She'd saved him from going back to Algeria, freed him from visa issues, and given him the time he needed to build up something amazing with Aylin.

He tried to call her on the way, but her phone was off. When he got there, the door was closed. He ran back to the reception, and the guy told him that she'd left the apartment the same day. The only thing she'd left was a letter for a certain Lewis.

"Lewis Alexis. That's me."

Everything that could be imagined had joined to strengthen his pessimism. His legs felt numb. He took the letter and left the building. Aylin had left for a reason. The friends he'd trusted must have told her already. That was the first assumption he made. He sat down on the ground and opened the envelope. His hands were shaking.

Congratulations!

I never thought you could do this to me. You promised to tell me everything. You promised! You betrayed me. I told you to go get married. I made that sacrifice, but not that you should do it behind my back. I guess you have what you need now. Of course you chose the easiest way.

Don't you know how hard it is to be lied to? How hard it is to be told the truth by someone else? My other half just got married. You broke my heart. You've destroyed every bit of it.

I'm leaving the country. I finished my exams, and I have no reason for staying here any longer. Please don't try to contact me. Don't try to follow me. I wish you all the best.

I love you.

Aylin

His body felt like jelly. He felt as if he'd been plunged in a frozen ocean and exposed to the coldest polar winds. He felt his body decaying. He fought against himself. He'd thought he was clever enough to win that war. He found out that his inner self was the main cause of all his worries. He'd certainly lost the value, the importance of his own existence. Everything now was trivial, temporary.

All he wished for ever since was death.

I don't know whether I'd say yes to death if it ever comes to take me away. What if I get the chance to meet it? I'll certainly be scared and shit my pants, but—and there's no doubt about that—I don't think there could be anything scarier than life itself.

End